PRAISE FOR M. L. BUCHMAN

A fabulous soaring thriller.

— *TAKE OVER AT MIDNIGHT,* MIDWEST
BOOK REVIEW

Meticulously researched, hard-hitting, and suspenseful.

— *PURE HEAT,* PUBLISHERS WEEKLY,
STARRED REVIEW

Expert technical details abound, as do realistic military missions with superb imagery that will have readers feeling as if they are right there in the midst and on the edges of their seats.

— *LIGHT UP THE NIGHT,* RT REVIEWS, 4 1/2
STARS

Buchman has catapulted his way to the top tier of my favorite authors.

— FRESH FICTION

Nonstop action that will keep readers on the edge of their seats.

— *TAKE OVER AT MIDNIGHT,* LIBRARY JOURNAL

M L. Buchman's ability to keep the reader right in the middle of the action is amazing.

— LONG AND SHORT REVIEWS

The only thing you'll ask yourself is, "When does the next one come out?"

— *WAIT UNTIL MIDNIGHT,* RT REVIEWS, 4 STARS

The first...of (a) stellar, long-running (military) romantic suspense series.

— *THE NIGHT IS MINE,* BOOKLIST, "THE 20 BEST ROMANTIC SUSPENSE NOVELS: MODERN MASTERPIECES"

I knew the books would be good, but I didn't realize how good.

— NIGHT STALKERS SERIES, KIRKUS REVIEWS

Buchman mixes adrenalin-spiking battles and brusque military jargon with a sensitive approach.

— PUBLISHERS WEEKLY

13 times "Top Pick of the Month"

— NIGHT OWL REVIEWS

Tom Clancy fans open to a strong female lead will clamor for more.

— *DRONE*, PUBLISHERS WEEKLY

Superb! Miranda is utterly compelling!

— *BOOKLIST,* STARRED REVIEW

Miranda Chase continues to astound and charm.

— BARB M.

Escape Rating: A. Five Stars! OMG just start with *Drone* and be prepared for a fantastic binge-read!

— READING REALITY

The best military thriller I've read in a very long time. Love the female characters.

— *DRONE,* SHELDON MCARTHUR,
FOUNDER OF THE MYSTERY BOOKSTORE,
LA

THE COMPLETE NIGHT STALKERS WEDDING STORIES

A MILITARY ROMANCE STORY COLLECTION

M. L. BUCHMAN

SIGN UP FOR M. L. BUCHMAN'S NEWSLETTER TODAY

CONTENTS

Other works by M. L. Buchman: *(* - also in audio)*

Action-Adventure Thrillers

Dead Chef
One Chef!
Two Chef!

Miranda Chase
Drone*
Thunderbolt*
Condor*
Ghostrider*
Raider*
Chinook*
Havoc*
White Top*
Start the Chase*

Science Fiction / Fantasy

Deities Anonymous
Cookbook from Hell: Reheated
Saviors 101

Single Titles
Monk's Maze
the Me and Elsie Chronicles

Contemporary Romance

Eagle Cove
Return to Eagle Cove
Recipe for Eagle Cove
Longing for Eagle Cove
Keepsake for Eagle Cove

Love Abroad
Heart of the Cotswolds: England
Path of Love: Cinque Terre, Italy

Where Dreams
Where Dreams are Born
Where Dreams Reside
Where Dreams Are of Christmas*
Where Dreams Unfold
Where Dreams Are Written
Where Dreams Continue

Non-Fiction

Strategies for Success
Managing Your Inner Artist/Writer
Estate Planning for Authors*
Character Voice
Narrate and Record Your Own
Audiobook*

Short Story Series by M. L. Buchman:

Action-Adventure Thrillers

Dead Chef

Miranda Chase Origin Stories

Romantic Suspense

Antarctic Ice Fliers

US Coast Guard

Contemporary Romance

Eagle Cove

Other

Deities Anonymous (fantasy)

Single Titles

The Emily Beale Universe
(military romantic suspense)

The Night Stalkers
MAIN FLIGHT
The Night Is Mine
I Own the Dawn
Wait Until Dark
Take Over at Midnight
Light Up the Night
Bring On the Dusk
By Break of Day
Target of the Heart
Target Lock on Love
Target of Mine
Target of One's Own
NIGHT STALKERS HOLIDAYS
Daniel's Christmas*
Frank's Independence Day*
Peter's Christmas*
Christmas at Steel Beach
Zachary's Christmas*
Roy's Independence Day*
Damien's Christmas*
Christmas at Peleliu Cove

Henderson's Ranch
Nathan's Big Sky*
Big Sky, Loyal Heart*
Big Sky Dog Whisperer*
Tales of Henderson's Ranch*

Shadow Force: Psi
At the Slightest Sound*
At the Quietest Word*
At the Merest Glance*
At the Clearest Sensation*

White House Protection Force
Off the Leash*
On Your Mark*
In the Weeds*

Firehawks
Pure Heat
Full Blaze
Hot Point*
Flash of Fire*
Wild Fire
SMOKEJUMPERS
Wildfire at Dawn*
Wildfire at Larch Creek*
Wildfire on the Skagit*

Delta Force
Target Engaged*
Heart Strike*
Wild Justice*
Midnight Trust*

Emily Beale Universe Short Story Series
The Night Stalkers
The Night Stalkers Stories
The Night Stalkers CSAR
The Night Stalkers Wedding Stories
The Future Night Stalkers

Delta Force
Th Delta Force Shooters
The Delta Force Warriors

Firehawks
The Firehawks Lookouts
The Firehawks Hotshots
The Firebirds

White House Protection Force
Stories

Future Night Stalkers
Stories (Science Fiction)

The Emily Beale Universe
Reading Order Road Map

any series and any novel may be read stand-alone
(all have a complete heartwarming Happy Ever After)

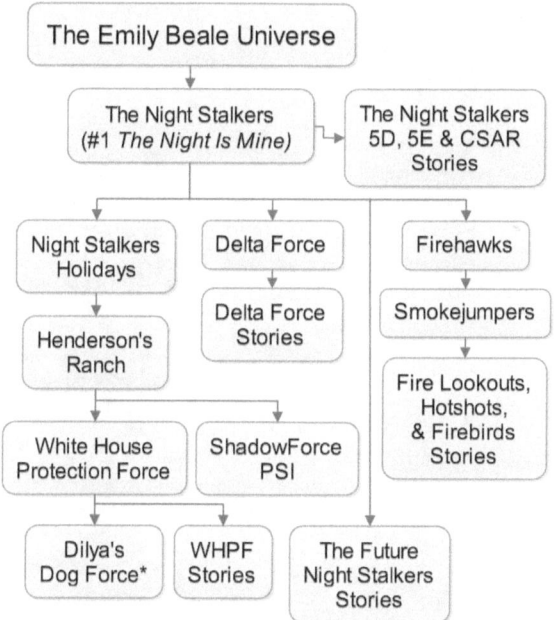

The Emily Beale Universe

The Night Stalkers (#1 *The Night Is Mine*)

The Night Stalkers 5D, 5E & CSAR Stories

Night Stalkers Holidays

Delta Force

Firehawks

Henderson's Ranch

Delta Force Stories

Smokejumpers

White House Protection Force

ShadowForce PSI

Fire Lookouts, Hotshots, & Firebirds Stories

Dilya's Dog Force*

WHPF Stories

The Future Night Stalkers Stories

* *Coming soon*

For more information and alternate reading orders, please visit: www.mlbuchman.com/reading-order

ABOUT THIS COLLECTION

THREE STORIES TO COMPLETE THE TALES.

"A Standout! A sugary treat for those who love romance." – *Publisher's Weekly, Ghost of Willow's Past*

The first three Night Stalkers novels ended before the happy-ever-after weddings were reached.

However, the path from true love to the altar is not always a smooth one. Come join the powerhouse women of the Night Stalkers as they wend their way toward the aisle.

PART I

NIGHT STALKERS WEDDINGS

In some of my series, especially my contemporary romances, I show the weddings. In others, typically my military romantic suspense, I rarely do.

Why?

I don't have a clear answer, mostly because I break the above rule too often. In the "Night Stalkers Holiday" series, we have two weddings in eight titles. In the "Night Stalkers Main Flight" the first wedding appears in Book #4, *Take Over at Midnight*. For this reason, Lola's wedding is not a short story, because it was already in the novel.

In fact, here's the funny joke. I set out to write a series of every wedding for every title in the Night Stalkers novels. It wasn't until I'd written and published the first three that I realized the wedding for #4 was already in the book. My creative brain managed to ignore that until I reopened *Take Over at Midnight* four years *after* its publication to begin researching Lola's wedding. It definitely took the wind out of my sails.

But it also fit. Emily, Kee, Connie, and Lola were the four women who launched the series and launched my career. When I started Emily's story, I was a typical hopeful writer, praying for someday success. By the time Lola's story was published seven years later, I was a full-time writer.

So here are the first three wedding stories. They encompass three of the original four books that were my concept for The Night Stalkers, back before I realized it would turn into a forty-two novel, seventy-story universe.

EMILY'S WEDDING

ABOUT THIS STORY

SHORTLY AFTER NIGHT STALKERS #1, THE NIGHT IS MINE...

Major Emily Beale of the US Army's Night Stalkers helicopter regiment found true love and the wedding looms imminent. But an emotional firestorm aims her toward a hard landing.

Major Mark Henderson knows she's the woman of his dreams, but he never considered that an aerial battle in the Hindu Kush ranked as a lower hazard mission than reaching the altar intact.

When her long-time friend the President decides to help, none of them may survive Emily's Wedding.

INTRODUCTION

EMILY IS CHILL.

That's how everyone remembers her after reading the books. That's how *I* remember her. But when I go back and reread her book, *The Night Is Mine,* she's a mess in so many fascinating ways as well.

How does a woman, who has fought to escape her mother's social world to forge her own path into the elite military of Special Operations Forces, become a married person? How can that work in her head?

Yes, she's fallen in love with Mark.

But her wedding day turned out nothing like I imagined. Yet it is perfectly her. In this story, I attempted to capture how she moved from the uncertainty of her role to become the mother-protector of all of the women who followed in her footsteps.

The answer? Even when she isn't chill, she is.

1

"No, you can't!" Emily Beale considered pounding her head against the small desk in the Bagram Airfield's USO communications center.

"Sure I can, *Squirt.*" Not a chance she'd give him the upper hand just because he used his childhood nickname for her.

"Listen to my words, *Sneaker Boy*. No! How complicated is that? Two whole letters and an exclamation point? Even you can understand that." Perhaps pounding the *phone* against the desk would be the right answer. She could feel her voice rising and couldn't stop it.

If only the wedding had happened months ago when it was supposed to. But their planned leave had been interrupted by a crisis mission, then another. Now their current deployment was ending and she didn't care who she had to kill, her marriage was going ahead.

"I'm the Commander-in-Chief. Of course I can do a wedding ceremony."

"Actually, Mr. President, you can't. That power *doesn't*

9

come with the office!" As soon as she shouted the words into the phone, she knew it was a mistake.

Until that moment, the other military around her had been chatting away with their own spouses, parents, children—whoever they were willing to spend their precious phone-home minutes with.

Now there was an echoing silence up and down the long rows of tiny desks at the Pat Tillman Memorial USO Center's phone bank. Each station was about as wide as her fiancé's shoulders—who thankfully was nowhere to be seen —with an empty ammo can for a seat. The whole reason she'd come over here to return this call, rather than doing it from the hangar, had been the privacy. She didn't want every single Night Stalker she flew with to overhear this.

Instead, every single person in the Tillman USO was looking at her with varying stages of shock on their face. They were mostly Air Force today, so they didn't really matter, but not even Special Operations majors were supposed to be chewing out the Commander-in-Chief. She'd always had special dispensation: President Peter Matthews had been the dashing older boy next door and also the only friend of Emily's overly precocious childhood. But these fliers didn't know that and she'd just kicked the base's gossip mill into high gear. Thankfully it couldn't get much worse.

Peter was still effusing in the background, "We'll have the ceremony here in The Residence, in the Blue Room. It will be great."

Emily lowered her voice and whispered through gritted teeth. "We're getting married on Mark's family ranch, *not* the White House." Her attempts to hide her frustration still had absolutely everyone's attention. And her whisper seemed to echo about the room.

"There a problem here?" A deep voice sounded close behind her. So much for not getting worse.

Emily didn't bother to turn her head. She placed her forehead on the desk and tried not to whimper.

"Hey, honey," Mark's big warm hand rested on her shoulder. "Who you talking to?"

She didn't bother to answer. Instead she simply held the phone up behind her head and he took it from her.

"Who'm I talkin' to?" Mark used his totally lame Texas accent rather than his most-decorated-Night Stalkers-helicopter-commander voice. He was from Montana, but never seemed to quite remember that.

Emily waited through The President's half of the conversation.

"W'all howdy there, Pete. What were you two jawin' about?"

Emily, head still down, gave her fiancé the finger. She could hear the whispers to either side of her as flyboys and girls started telling their spouses about the crazy woman yelling at the Commander-in-Chief. Yelling? Next time she saw him, she was going to dump him into the Reflecting Pool—a second time. Just like when he was eighteen and she'd been a furious twelve that he was leaving for college without her. Back then it had upset the park police. This time she wouldn't care if it upset the Secret Service.

"Now, Peter..." Thankfully the Texas was gone and Mark was trying to sound calm and placating.

He had long since learned the mayhem she could unleash if riled—especially since he was here and her target was most of seven thousand miles away. *Most of?* Now Mark had *her* doing Texas. She raised her head just enough to thump it back down on the desk. The cool wood did nothing to abate the heat roaring between her ears.

"I'm afraid Emily is right. That power is not granted with the office."

"Uh-huh..."

"Uh-huh..."

"Well, you know, sir, they've got that online church where you can get ordained in just a couple minutes. Just sign yourself up and then it's all fair and square..."

Emily tried to jolt up in protest and bumped against Mark. The man was so solid that she practically bounced off. Resigned to her doom, she returned to her head-down position. *Duck and cover!*

"No, we've got our heart set on my family's ranch... Montana, that's right. When was your last vacation, sir? The day after Election Day? Not much of a break. W'all..."

And...the Texas was back.

"Don'cher think it's 'bout time yer took un?"

Except Mark's Texas might have been Virginia with a little bit of Scotland mixed in. It would be easier to accept if he didn't think it was so endearing—which would be kind of cute, if it wasn't so awful.

"Wonderful! I'll let my folks know that Frank will be calling."

The head of the Presidential Protection Detail was just going to be *so* happy about this.

"Do you want to speak some more with Emily?"

"No? Well, can't say as I blame you. But you're gonna owe me some, 'cause I 'spect I'm about to catch a bellyful. Goodbye, sir!"

He reached past her to hang up the phone.

"Don't see what has you all fussed up, honey. He's just—"

Emily shot back an elbow square into his hard gut, which earned her little more than a surprised grunt. One of these days she'd catch him when he wasn't ready. She stood up to face him, doing her best to ignore the dozen eavesdroppers.

"What was that for, darlin'?" He grinned down. Being so damn handsome wasn't going to save him this time.

Maybe another tactic. She pulled him down into a kiss —an unusual enough event on a military base to make sure she had everyone's attention, but she was past caring. Catcalls and loud whistles echoed about the room.

She felt Mark ease into the kiss.

That's when she fisted him in the solar plexus with a sharp right jab and took him to his knees.

"That was dirty," he gasped for air but his body wasn't going to cooperate for a minute or two.

"You should understand by now," she recalled the t-shirt that her father had given her when she'd earned her Taekwondo Black Belt in high school. "I fight like a girl."

2

IT WAS THE COMPANY'S FIRST TASTE OF AMERICA AFTER A SIX-month deployment. They hit Joint Base Lewis-McChord with the sunrise after a twenty-three hour flight. The cool and moist September air a vast relief after flying through an Afghan summer—blazing with heat and near constant firefights. Summer and fall were the seasons of war over there and he was glad to be out of it for a while.

Because they were the 5th Battalion D Company and always ready—even when promised a full week of uninterrupted leave—they took care of their helicopters the first moment after touchdown on American soil.

The War in Afghanistan had to end some day, but Mark wasn't seeing any obvious signs of it doing that yet. Especially not for SOF. Special Operations Forces like Delta Force, the Army Rangers, and the fliers of the 160th SOAR were still deep there.

So, putting first things first, they immediately unloaded their helos from the belly of the C-5 Galaxy transport plane. The helicopters were reassembled, refueled, test-flown, and hangared before Mark dismissed the team.

Then they'd all piled into vans to head up to Sea-Tac Airport.

It might have been poor planning that there was a two-hour wait for the next flight to Great Falls, Montana, or good planning as it was lunchtime. That, and the fact that the US allowed bars in their airports. Perhaps if he hadn't bought the first couple rounds...

But in Mark's opinion it was his job as commander to encourage his people in battle. And it was just as much his responsibility to encourage them on the ground.

Besides, the Concourse C bar was as close to a bachelor party as he was going to get. Somehow, doing it up in a dry country like Afghanistan, on an airbase, while living in body armor around the clock, didn't quite cut it.

They were a pretty loose crowd by the time they rolled out of the bar and reached the gate.

"We would like," the gate agent finally announced, "to invite those with small children or needing extra time to board the flight to please come forward. We'd also like to welcome any veterans currently serving in the US Armed Forces to board at this time."

Once the women and children were clear, the 5D stormed the queue.

Thankfully the flight was half empty, so they simply took possession of the rear of the aircraft. The stews were wisely routing any passengers with far back seats to open positions further forward. The Dash 8 was a small plane, just two narrow seats to either side, and the 5D took more than its fair share of them. There was no way for guys as broad-shouldered as Tim Maloney and his best buddy Big John Wallace to fit in the two seats side by side.

Eventually, he could feel them closing the baggage hold's doors by the solid thumps transmitted up his heels.

They were too loud as a group to hear any announcements, so Mark moved along, shoving them down into seats.

Once he had them all down—he'd leave it to the stews to make sure they were buckled in—Mark dropped into his seat beside Emily. She was staring out the window as they were pushed back from the gate and beginning engine startup.

"Yer mighty quiet there, darlin'!"

She gave him one of *those* looks.

"What's wrong, honey?" He dropped the Texas then reached out and took her hand as Tim and John started setting up some kind of a game with the flight attendants. The prizes being the little packets of pretzels and peanuts. Mark knew the game would be rigged to move the maximum number of them into the 5D's hands and that the stews would never see it coming. A couple of the attendants were seriously cute and he wondered if there might not be a few more guests for the wedding before the flight was over. He could hear the guys working on it. *Only a two-hour flight, boys. Better be quick about it.*

Mark didn't need to play such games anymore. He had Emily Beale. He could never get over how incredible it felt to hold her hand. It wasn't just the connection that coursed through his system; it also humbled him every time, that *he* was the one who got to do it. Though she returned the gesture, she didn't turn from her study out the window as they taxied to the active runway. It all seemed to be in slow motion after six months in Bagram. No one trying to mortar them on the runway here. No yelling, no running soldiers. These people behaved as if there wasn't a war on. He knew the disorienting feeling wasn't going to wear off any time soon, so he ignored it and focused on the wonder of holding Emily's hand.

"Not having second thoughts, are you?" The sole beer that he'd allowed himself wasn't enough to keep his throat from going dry at the thought.

She shook her head and the straight fall of her golden-blonde hair swirled about her shoulders. Her hand tightened in his.

"Then cheer up, Emma," his nickname for her while they'd been working undercover inside the White House. "It's only a life sentence after all."

At that she turned to him. "Thank God for that." She kissed him on the shoulder, which was sweet but didn't do much to heat up the fire that he always had simmering for her. There was no sign of tears in those perfect sky-blue eyes, but then there never were—well, almost never. She kept those to herself except for the few times he'd been really thoughtless.

"Something's eating at you."

She nodded absently—either agreement or just an acknowledgement that he'd said something, he couldn't tell —then turned to face once more out the window.

Mark kept his sigh to himself. That's what he got for falling in love with Emily Beale. The woman never spoke a single thought until she was good and ready to.

Before he could pursue it, Dusty James called out to him. "Hey Mark. You got to tell these fools that Portland, Oregon is not the end of the Earth."

"You sure about that?" He made a point of leaning out and looking back then furrowing his brow. "I always thought it was."

"Man!" Dusty groaned in frustration. He was always trying to defend his home state and Mark was the only other one in the 5D who'd actually been there. His sole excursion was due to a hot little brunette named Jennine he'd met on leave a couple years back.

She'd promised him sex on a sandy Pacific Ocean beach that stretched for miles. Of course she failed to mention that the wind never dropped below twenty knots and the air rarely warmed over sixty degrees in a chill sea fog—all of which she seemed to think was normal for July. The summer ocean invited him to swim, but she warned him of rip tides and hypothermia risks—locals never swam in it. The total fiasco was finalized when her parents—not being stupid—had put them in separate rooms. Oregon had a beautiful wildness, which Jennine had been willing to share for all the good it hadn't done them. Maybe both were best left to the imagination.

"I'm pretty sure that Oregon exists only in some parallel universe, Dustman. You find a girl there, you're welcome to her."

Dusty continued protesting as the others sought a new target to tease.

Mark faced front as the pilot eased the throttles forward and the plane slipped down the runway. Even that felt wrong. Bagram takeoffs were full throttle, hold down the nose wheel until long past take-off speed was achieved, then pop up into a hard climb to get out of RPG range, because rocket-propelled grenades could ruin a man's day.

So many things were disorienting.

His past filled with mostly meaningless women was now...the past as well. Two more days and he'd be a married man. She was nothing like his quiet, endlessly patient half-Cheyenne mother, who'd always been his measure for women.

Emily Beale was strong-headed, taciturn, and always showing a cool facade—until the moment she tipped over into pure, unadulterated lethal. He'd never wanted anyone, *needed* anyone the way he needed Emily. What was up with that? It didn't sound like any Major Mark Henderson that he knew.

For life.

He believed in that. It's what his parents had. He'd just never imagined it for himself.

Maybe he understood Emily's strange mood as the plane eased off the runway and began its long climb.

3
_____

IT WAS EARLY THE NEXT MORNING, AND EMILY KNEW SHE'D have a psychotic break if she didn't get away from everyone for a while. The boys had spent the previous afternoon, after their arrival at the ranch, wearing themselves out with a touch football game that ended up with more tackles than touches. Dinner had been a grand affair at a campfire out behind the main house filled with pilots, crew chiefs, and ranch guests.

Mac and Ama, Mark's parents, had made her welcome. But she still didn't fit in. In any group, she'd always been—

"Here you go," Doug, the ranch's stable manager, led a big horse the color of mahogany out of one of the stalls and handed her the reins, as if she knew what to do with a horse. Then he pushed a straw cowboy hat onto of her head, as if she knew what to do with a cowboy hat.

She'd mentioned to Mark that she wanted to get away and he'd suggested they go for a ride. A ride? What did she know about riding? She was the daughter of the FBI Director and a socialite mother. She'd grown up in the heart of D.C. No cowboy hats.

Doug led another horse over to Mark, which was an even taller pure black mount. Mark already had his cowboy hat on, which looked both unfamiliar and utterly charming. If he'd taken off his mirrored shades, she might not have even recognized him.

Emily looked at her horse. It looked back at her. Détente.

"Here," Doug returned and broke off a three-inch piece of a carrot he must have hidden in his pocket. "Flat hand, thumb tucked back as far as you can. A horse isn't nasty, at least not Chesapeake, but she can't see what she's eating, so let's not feed her any confusing fingers." He dropped the carrot in her open hand, then guided it over to the horse. The soft brush of Chesapeake's lips across her palm tickled. She rubbed the horse's soft nose and decided that the carrot-crunching sounds were soothing.

"Thanks. I can do this."

"Of course you can. Easier than flying a Black Hawk helicopter." Doug showed her how to mount. "Always from the left."

She'd just remember that it was the opposite of a Black Hawk. In military Black Hawks a pilot sat on the right side, but now she was back to the left side—copilot to a horse.

Once Doug had the stirrups adjusted, he gestured side to side with the reins, "Right and left rudder." He grabbed her boot and moved her foot through a kicking gesture into the horse's side. "Collective up." He moved her hands and reins forward, "Cyclic forward." Then he pulled the reins back into her lap.

Chesapeake took a step backward just the way a helicopter would until she eased off the reins again.

"That's collective down and cyclic back. More pressure

21

equals a bigger response, so letting loose the reins and kick hard equals go fast."

If only she could explain what she was feeling so clearly, but she couldn't put words to it.

"Horses are emotional. Command with confidence— which should be no trouble for you—and the horse will behave."

Emily nodded once to Doug in thanks, a second time to herself to anchor the lesson, then she eased off the reins and experimentally thumped her boot heels into Chesapeake's ribs. The horse shifted up through a walk to a trot. She eased back on the reins just a little, and the horse settled into the trot without going up to one of its faster speeds.

Together, she and Chesapeake trotted out of the shadowed barn and into the bright morning light. The day was warm and the sun felt good, as if it was somehow scorching away little flakes of her strange mood. More would be better.

"C'mon, Mark," Emily called back as they trotted past the corrals, discovering that twisting in her saddle could turn the horse as well. "What's holding you up?"

Mark's muttered curse did her heart some good. That she was out past the ranch buildings and nearly over the first rise before he caught up with her, made her feel even cheerier.

"Is there anything you aren't amazing at, woman?" Mark trotted up beside her.

"Had a good teacher."

"I thought you'd never ridden."

"Let's find out," Emily eased the reins, but wasn't comfortable kicking her horse. It seemed like a nasty trick to pull on a perfectly nice horse. Instead she leaned forward and whispered, "Let's go, girl."

In moments the horse's rhythm change from jouncy to fast and smooth, like riding the natural glide slope of an auto-rotate descent. The wind snatched her hair back from her face and the prairie grass began rushing by. She risked reaching up to check her hat, but it was a snug fit and wasn't going anywhere. She leaned into the wind and in the process eased the reins some more.

Chesapeake lowered her head and they flew across the ground.

She heard a soft, "Shit!" from somewhere far behind her.

She'd always wondered what it felt like to fly *outside* of the helicopter and, for the first time, she received a taste of it. No wonder cowboys always whooped when galloping in the movies. She let one fly as they crested the soft roll of the grassy ridge.

Emily had visited the ranch a few times on leave, but this was her first time when there wasn't snow on the ground. And she'd certainly never seen it from horseback.

The view was breathtaking—that and the roaring wind of the gallop which ripped away her gasp of amazement. She sat up slowly and eased back on the reins. Just as Doug had promised, down on the collective, ease back on the cyclic and Chesapeake eased from race to trot and finally mosey. She finally understood what the word truly meant— a lazy side-to-side roll as the horse eased to a walk and huffed out a happy breath. Emily thumped her alongside her neck in what she hoped was a sisterly pat.

"We'll have to do more of that later, won't we?" She'd take the horse twitching her ears back to listen in her direction as agreement.

At a mosey she could appreciate the landscape that had opened out in front of her when she'd crested the ridge. The sharp mountains of the Montana Front Range broke skyward with a visceral power she could feel in her gut. The lower foothills harbored clumps of dark conifers as well as maple and birch just starting into their fall plumage. The prairie was carpeted with yellow coneflower, sprinkled with multi-colored anemones, and accented by nodding columbine. She loved columbine.

"That's my wedding bouquet!" Emily waved a hand at the wild colors of the prairie as Mark finally caught up with her. She wished she could capture the dark mountains and the blue sky that went on forever as well. She tipped way back in the saddle to look straight up from beneath her hat. "No wonder they call it the Big Sky."

"Kind of amazing, isn't it?"

"How did we not ride out here before?"

"Six months in Afghanistan. Or did you already forget?"

Emily could only smile at Mark. For a moment, she had. The lush Montana landscape had painted over the ochre Afghan desert imprinted inside her.

They rode down the far side of the ridge in a comfortable silence. Crested another ridge. Descended through a thick copse of trees, and out the far side they rode up to a stream. Once again the land was carpeted in flowers.

"Must have rained in the last week or so to make this," Mark eased to a stop along the stream. It was twenty-feet wide and looked to be a couple feet deep. A darker patch lay along one side.

"This your fishing hole?"

"One of them," Mark sounded like a man in paradise.

Emily let herself look at him—look at Major Mark Henderson and think the word *husband*. It was a good thought. He was the best man she knew and, much to her surprise, she loved him.

She dismounted and went to stand close by the burbling water.

4

———

MARK TRIED TO FIGURE OUT WHAT HE'D DONE RIGHT IN THIS life, or any other life for that matter, that Emily stood waiting for him. For *him*.

He slid to the ground and came up behind her, folding her into his arms.

"What's bugging you, babe? I know something—"

She turned in his arms and put a finger on his lips.

"Not here. Not now. It's too perfect." Then without shifting her gaze from his, she eased down to the grass, tugging him down after her. There was no need to tell him twice.

They'd made love in a hospital bed and in the back of a Black Hawk. A Forward Operating Base in Afghanistan hadn't afforded much more than stolen moments in dark corners. Last night after the big cookout, everyone had stayed up late telling campfire stories. Tim had sweet-talked one of the flight attendants to keep him company. Not to be outdone, Big John had sidled up to a particularly curvy New York stockbroker who'd come to the ranch with three girlfriends to get over a recent breakup. By the time Emily led Mark to bed, Afghanistan jet lag had overtaken their plans and crashed them into sleep.

Now there was just the horses, the wide prairie, and the most amazing woman he'd ever met.

He tugged off his hat.

"Uh-uh, cowboy. Keep the hat."

"Wa'll," if she wanted a cowboy to make love to her, he could arrange that. "Ah guess that ah'll jes—"

"Lose the accent and the shirt."

He was too wise a man to argue. Mark did raise her up to slip his shirt beneath her. Next time he'd remember a blanket. As she lay back, she tugged off her blouse as well. She was an impossible combination of womanly curves and a sleek strength that only a career soldier could ever possess. The two together stole his words and he did his best to show just how much he appreciated that she'd said yes all those months ago.

Emily rose for him, just as she had that very first time, as if every moment was a new discovery of wonder. He'd never tire of evoking that deep response from her. He loved that he could drive her out of that perfect control she showed even in the fiercest firefight.

As he eased off her boots and jeans he imagined how the other guys must picture Emily making love. The cool, almost emotionless blonde—always in perfect control. Wouldn't they be surprised to know that she groaned at his lightest touch. And when he did something just right, she even begged.

The cool blonde was for others. The best lover of his entire life was for him alone.

Now both naked except for their cowboy hats (and his jeans trapped down on his cowboy boots), he worked his way up her glorious body, wondering if the team would care if the bride and groom didn't show up for the wedding. They'd stay here. He held himself over her for a moment and looked down to admire them coming together. It was the most amazing thing to see their two bodies join so completely. He didn't want this to be just one moment. Maybe later he'd sneak back to the ranch for a blanket and some food, and they'd stay here making love until—

Emily flailed an arm upward catching him across the chin, snapping his jaw shut—hard.

"Yow! My tong-ah!"

"Cut it out, Chesapeake!" Emily flailed one of those long perfect arms over her head while she lay in the grass, but managed to miss his face this time. "I said shoo! Don't eat my hat, you dumb horse."

Mark looked up, ready to slap the horse's nose. Hell of a moment to interrupt. He supported himself with one hand so that he could strike with the other.

It wasn't Chesapeake. It wasn't even Wind Runner, his own mount.

For a moment he couldn't make sense of what he saw.

Then it clicked into focus.

With a cry, he attempted to rear back. He made it to his feet, but with his ankles trapped in his bunched jeans, he had no control. He kept going and flailed over backward to splash down into the deep stream.

It was cold enough to shrivel him for life!

5

ONE MOMENT EMILY WAS READY TO DIE OF CONTENTMENT.
Mark was an incredible lover. And watching his body poised
over hers against the sun-brilliant blue of the Montana sky
only made him look all the more perfect. Each time he filled
her, it was a completion that she never imagined possible.
Their bodies had been designed for this perfect moment of
coming together—the opening and welcoming, the taking
in, the completion.

Mark had so stoked her need for him, that the tug on
her hat had barely distracted her. The events building
toward the wedding had only compounded that ten times
more. She was so desperate for him that it had been an
automatic gesture to brush Chesapeake aside—no more.

Mark's cry of alarm at the horse trying to eat her hat
would have shocked her if she hadn't been so anticipating
the next moment.

Then he rose up like...she didn't know what. Did grizzly
bears look like that? Tall, magnificent against the blue sky,
muscular, and gloriously aroused.

No. But maybe a panicked *Homo sapiens* did. Except for the gloriously aroused part.

He disappeared out of sight. There was a huge splash, and cold water sprinkled over her body, like fresh rain on a hot afternoon.

Enough of her brain returned from anticipating Mark inside her for her to wonder what had alarmed him so.

She slowly tipped her head back, until she was looking at just who was tugging on her hat. It wasn't Chesapeake. It wasn't Wind Runner.

For one thing, it had a broad, black face that even upside down was the wrong shape. It also had curving horns that stuck out of either side of its head by several feet—ending in wicked-looking points.

It stared at her for a moment with one liquid-brown eye, blinked with incredibly long lashes, and then inspected her with the other.

Then it turned away to graze on the flowers.

"That's my wedding bouquet you're eating, you know."

"Lucy!" a woman's voice called. "There you are."

Emily sat up enough to see what was really going on. A woman with shiny-blonde hair rode out of the red-tinged trees. Her horse was a patchwork like spilled black paint spilled on a white canvas.

"Sorry to disturb your sunbathing. Lucy's a bit of an escape artist."

"Sunbathing?" No, she'd been on the verge of— Emily spotted Mark. He was still in the stream. He was halfway out of the water, but a bush blocked the woman's view of him. He eased back down into the water. Well, she wasn't going to be so frail. "It is a nice day for it."

She reached for her shirt, then thought better of it. It

was snarled beneath her along with Mark's and if she straightened out one, she'd reveal the other.

The woman, just a few years Emily's junior, rode up to the monstrous cow, and slapped it on the butt with a coiled rope. "Home, Lucy." The cow looked at her balefully for a moment, then began ambling down along the stream. "Sorry for the trouble. This is Clarence," she introduced her horse first which was maybe what all true cowgirls did. "I'm Julie from the ranch next door."

"Emily, from this ranch, I guess. That's Chesapeake," she waved a negligent hand as if she was sitting in her armor in a Night Stalkers' briefing room, not naked among the columbines.

"Emily. The one marrying the son of the ranch?"

"Tomorrow night."

"Always good to get in some sunbathing and relaxing before something like that."

"It is," Emily agreed wondering just how surreal this conversation was going to get. It was now far too late to grab for her shirt without looking like a complete fool.

"Suppose I ought to warn you, that stream water is glacier fed. Just wouldn't want you to jump in not knowing that." Julie nodded over toward where Wind Runner had grazed around out of Emily's immediate sight. Her wry smile indicated that she hadn't missed a single thing of what was going on.

Emily fished out her shirt and tugged it on, tossing Mark's a little closer to the water. Actually, too close. It cleared the bank and plopped into the stream. He snagged it as it floated by, then sent her a fulminating look.

"Thanks for the warning," Emily expected she could get to like Clarence and Julie-from-the-ranch-next-door. That gave her some hope. She didn't have a maid of honor, but sitting here, still mostly naked on the very prickly grass, and asking a total stranger cowgirl to step in didn't seem the right answer either.

"You have a good time, y'hear?" Julie turned her horse with thoughtless ease.

"I always try," Emily called after her.

"She gone?" Mark whispered through chattering teeth.

Emily thought about the story she'd be telling around the campfire tonight, her pre-wedding night, and couldn't help herself. For perhaps the first time in her life she actually giggled. Maybe she'd take Julie's advice and enjoy herself a bit.

"Not yet," Julie and Lucy the cow were nowhere to be seen. Emily dressed and began picking her wedding bouquet. She had it mostly assembled before she called the all clear.

6

———

"So there we were. Mark fishing, me reading my book, because, I mean, ick!"

Mark wondered what had come over Emily. She was never a storyteller, but tonight she was ruling the campfire. But of all stories to tell... At least she was changing it for the better.

With the sun set and darkness down, the fire lit her face with a warm glow. Everyone crowded in close, rapt with attention.

"Then the biggest cow I've ever seen—huge horns, I mean out like this," she spread her arms to their limits, sticking out her index fingers like the points he'd thought were going to gore him, "—came up from behind and took a taste of my hat."

"What did you do?" Of course Tim was the perfect audience, being an accomplished storyteller himself.

Mark was just glad that the ranch guests were off at some other event tonight, so it was just the 5D's crews around the fire. It hadn't been his finest moment.

"I might have yelped and I definitely lost my place in my

book. But it's what Mark did that makes it all so perfect." Emily held onto his arm as if he was the conquering hero.

"Faced down a longhorn for you?" Tim guessed.

"Wrangled him to the ground," Big John tried to one-up him.

"Fileted the beast with a fishing knife."

John slapped his palms together, "Longhorn steaks for the wedding feast tomorrow. Yes!"

"My man..." Emily drew it out. "My man squealed like a little girl and fell head over heels into the glacier stream!"

"No! Wait!" Mark's protest was too little too late.

Everyone was laughing and he couldn't seem to shout the truth down—even if it was the only bit of truth in the whole tale.

He had intended to race to her rescue, but he'd resurfaced just in time to see the perfectly cool, and brilliantly naked, Emily shoo the monster cow off as if it was just an overgrown kitten. By the time Julie from across the road was gone, he'd been far too cold to resume any amorous intent. Pulling up those icy jeans had been one of the hardest things he'd done in a long time. They should add that to the Night Stalkers Green Platoon testing.

Mark tried to think of some way this could be more embarrassing when a big hand landed on his shoulder.

He turned to see the firelight illuminating Frank Adams' face. The head of the President's Protection Detail clamped down on him hard.

"Thought you promised to take care of this lady, Major Henderson?" The threat of retribution was clear in his tone and his crushing hold.

"Hi, Frank," Emily jumped to her feet and gave Frank a solid hug, which thankfully forced Frank to release his viselike grip on Mark's shoulder.

What in the world had gotten into her tonight?

"Where's your boss?"

"That's the greeting I get?" Frank grumbled. "Everyone cares about the Main Man, not about me." But he held Emily close and gently for a long moment which made Mark forgive him most anything.

Mark rose and traded a firm handshake with him. There was some test of strength there, but nothing he couldn't handle. No real point in trying, when Emily had taken both of them down more than once on her own. They might be the best at what they did, but Emily was in a whole other category.

"The advance team has already been through the place. But your parents are hitching a ride on Air Force One, so the President figured arriving tomorrow for the wedding was better than today."

"He actually got something right," Emily agreed. "Nice change."

Frank looked pained at the insult to the Commander-in-Chief, but knew better than to contradict Emily.

Mark found him a beer and they all sat back down around the fire. They tapped their bottles together in a silent toast to an amazing woman—at least that's what he was toasting.

"So," Frank's big voice silenced the circle. "What's this about you squealing like a little girl, Major Henderson?"

Mark just groaned.

7

_____

EMILY WAITED ALONE IN THE RANCH'S FOREYARD. WELL, JUST her and Frank. She knew other agents were spread throughout the ranch, but they were keeping a low profile.

Mark was still out, which didn't surprise her after how they'd spent most of the night. It might not have been a sunny meadow by a burbling stream, but he had made her last night as a single woman *very* memorable. How different married sex would feel, she supposed that she'd find out tonight.

What *was* surprising was that *she* was awake—had barely slept.

"It's not nerves." But Emily still didn't know what it had been.

"You sure?" She'd forgotten Frank beside her, part of his Secret Service stealth mode.

"Shut up, Frank."

"Then don't talk to yourself aloud, Major Beale."

"What about you, Frank? Were you nervous?"

That earned her a grunt that said it wasn't that simple.

"Well, it's not nerves."

"Whatever you say, Major."

She spotted three dark dots against the blue sky.

"Personal relationships are one of the President's *very few* blind spots," Frank sounded defensive as he nodded toward that dots that were rapidly expanding into the green-and-white Marine Corps helicopters assigned to HMX-1. "I wouldn't look for any real useful counseling there if something's bothering you."

"Shit. Am I that transparent?"

"Not a chance, Emily," he said her name softly for one of the few times in their acquaintance. "But I've been married a long time and... Well, I'm..."

"I've met Beatrice. You're the thoughtful and sensitive one in the relationship."

Frank shrugged uncomfortably.

"Makes you all the better, Frank."

"Thank you, Major." And that brief crack in the door was closed again.

In shared silence, they watched as the helicopters resolved into White Hawks—Black Hawk helicopters re-engineered and armored to carry the President. They were called "White Tops" for the white upper section of their paint job.

After seven years flying the Black Hawk airframe, the heavy thrum of the rotors sounded like home to her. Just as the lead helo touched down in the main yard, Mark came stumbling out of the house half dressed: his pants buckled, but his shirt in his hand, and his hair still a mess. He blinked hard against the bright morning light, found his mirrored shades and eased them on, still shirtless. A phalanx of flying Black Hawks would ring a full mission alert alarm right through a Night Stalker's deepest sleep.

Mark was so beautiful it was ridiculous, not that she was complaining.

The door on the helo opened. Her oldest friend stepped down, closely followed by her father and mother. All three of them were looking at Mark.

President Peter Matthews laughed.

Her father offered his amused, enigmatic FBI Director smile that could mean anything.

Her mother's sigh of dismay was almost audible despite the helo's engines still winding down.

8
———

EMILY WAS UNSURE IF SHE WAS HAPPY, OR FRUSTRATED AT HOW quickly the morning had passed.

Mark's parents had led the way through the ranch buildings to an idyllic spot. There was a big swimming hole, or perhaps it was a small lake, in a low spot beyond the guest cabins. The still water reflected the blue sky, all protected by a soft-sloped, grassy berm. A dock with a low diving board reached out from one side. To the other was the platform for a gazebo that presently made a natural stage, extending partly over the water. The structure of the gazebo itself wouldn't be built until spring, but the platform was perfect beneath the sunny sky, appearing to float on the water.

With the entire 5D available, except Tim who was presently driving his stewardess back to the airport, seats were set up and arranged in moments. Ama, Mark's mother, sent them out onto the prairie with buckets of water to collect more flowers.

"Daniel apologizes for not coming," Peter showed up close beside her as she watched the activity helplessly from the top of the berm. "But he wants to know if you made the wedding cake. If you did, I promised to bring him back a piece."

"Wedding cake?" She blinked in confusion. Looking around the grassy slope, she didn't see any food. Hadn't thought of any wedding cake.

"Well, whoever makes it, he'll still be sorry he missed this."

"I—" she tried to make sense of what was going on. Seventy-two hours ago, she'd been flying her last patrol along the Arandu arms-smuggling route out of Pakistan. And now she was being asked about wedding cakes. She had her dress blues in her duffle, but that was as far as her thinking had gone.

"You okay, Squirt? Something bothering you?"

"I thought something was off last night, too," Frank said softly from close by her shoulder.

"You *are* looking kinda peaked," Big John rumbled out. He was even bigger than Frank. His hands so big that the bucket of flowers he was carrying looked like a child's toy.

"Nerves," Dusty declared, then blew his macho by sniffing at the flowers he'd collected. "Gotta remember for the future that ladies like these kinds of things."

"Who's your maid of honor?" Tim was back.

"You!" Emily turned and shouted in his face. "I'm putting you in a goddamn flower print dress and making you hold my bouquet when it happens! Do you see any other women here?"

And there it was.

She didn't know if she wanted to scream or cry or shoot someone—anyone.

This whole circle of men were looking at her in abashed silence, not understanding a thing.

Emily stormed away. For lack of anywhere better to go, she went down to the horse barn and found Chesapeake. She didn't have a carrot, but the horse seemed content with a nose rub.

"How about you? You want to be this girl's only girl friend?"

Her whole life had been navigating the role of being a lone female among men. Her father's friends had been other male FBI agents. Her mother's friends had been the social vortex of D.C. and couldn't be more foreign, or less appealing, to Emily than if they were all from Neptune—a Martian she could deal with. At West Point, women had been few and far between. There were only three other women who flew the 101st Airborne when she had been there. And she was the first, and still the only, woman in the Night Stalkers.

This afternoon she was going through the ultimate right of passage for a woman, her own wedding for crap's sake. And she didn't have a clue what to do or what she was supposed to be feeling. Was there any kind of normal any more? Would there ever be again?

"Emily?"

She sighed and rested her cheek against Chesapeake's coarse hide. She smelled good, like the fresh hay she'd almost been made love to in yesterday. "What Mom?"

"We've never understood each other."

No point in agreeing with simple fact.

"You were always your father's daughter far more than you were mine."

Emily looked up at her mother. Helen Cartwright Magnuson Beale had bequeathed her slender frame and height to her daughter. Her father had given her the blue eyes that both attracted and scared men. Mom was so out of place in the shadowed barn, wearing a Donna Karan summer dress and her Ferragamo sandals with a Stuart Weitzman clutch. And how did she know all that? Some part of her mother's training had stuck despite Emily's best efforts to block it out.

"You know I hoped—"

Emily buried her face once more against Chesapeake's neck. She didn't need a lecture on the wonderful matches her mother had tried to make for her over the years with this and that social climber. She'd been very careful to never mention the President's crazy proposal, that she still didn't understand, because she knew it would break her mother's heart that Emily had turned him down.

"But Mark—"

"Mom..." Emily ground it out as a warning.

"But Mark," she put on her full-on D.C. hostess tone commanding Emily's silence, "clearly loves you so much that I couldn't wish anyone else for you."

That had Emily jerking around to face her. Chesapeake did the same.

"Oh honey. You can see it plain as day on both of you. You must know that about the man."

She nodded. She did. She nodded harder.

"Then what's the problem?"

Emily waved a helpless hand. "You said it. I'm my father's daughter. I might as well be his son for how feminine I am. I don't have a single female friend. I don't know how to be female. Or even what that means!"

Her throat choked closed and she swallowed hard, but knew her voice wasn't steady.

"I have no one to stand with me. No one to help me." She never needed anyone's help—yet suddenly she did.

"The friends will come later. You're too amazing a

woman for them not to come. And you will guide them and help them. That part of you is from being *my* daughter."

Then her mother took a step closer and tentatively reached a perfectly manicured hand across the gap between them to brush her fingertips along Emily's arm.

"As for today, I will stand with you, if you'll have me."

Emily could only blink in surprise. She'd always been merely a "marriageable commodity" to her mother, or so she'd thought. And now the quintessential woman of D.C. was telling her that she was an amazing woman herself.

She rested her rough and callused hand over her mother's for a long time before she could answer.

"I'd like that."

9

"You've got to be kidding me!" Mark stood atop the berm in his dress blues.

His father stood beside him, gray-haired, but still fitting neatly into his SEAL commander's whites. Mom wore her best dress, a simple, straight blue one that made her look wonderful beside her husband. The President and Frank stood to his other side, surveying the waiting crowd.

His father had close-mown a green aisle that led down the gentle slope. An impossible bounty of flowers lined the path to either side down to the clustered chairs and the gazebo platform that appeared to hover over the blue-sky reflection of the lake.

The pilots and crew chiefs of the 5D were all in their uniforms as well.

"This can't be happening!" No one argued with him.

Tim and Big John were acting as ushers.

And they'd seated every single person on the right-hand side of the aisle. The chairs for the groom's side of the open-air wedding were empty. Not even Doug or any of the other ranch hands were sitting on his side.

"Don't worry, son," his father thumped him on the back. "Your mother and I don't mind sitting alone." They both were clearly enjoying the joke.

He really didn't need this but, out of options, the five of them walked down the mown aisle to take their places at the very front of the ceremony. Every single person grinned at him from the bride's side of the aisle.

It shouldn't be a surprise. Of course they'd all be on Emily's side—in every sense of the word.

At the platform, he kissed his mom and shook his dad's hand before stepping up. That's what he'd focus on: the two of them. They had made it through so much. Dad's twenty years of service, innumerable deployments, and finally taking over the failing ranch and getting it back on its feet. With a woman like Emily beside him, he knew he could do anything too.

Now it was just he, Frank, and the President standing and waiting quietly over the shimmering lake. Whether it was the presence of the Commander-in-Chief or anticipation of the upcoming event, the crowd was speaking only in whispers.

"I guess you're the best man, Frank."

"Wondered when you'd figure that out, Major," Frank grinned at him. "I figure my main job is to kick your ass if you mess this up, which I promise you that I will do if necessary."

"Even my best man is on Emily's side," he tried to sound upset.

"Duh!" Frank wasn't helping matters. "You've got the ring?"

Mark handed over the small box carefully so that he didn't do something stupid like drop it in the lake.

Frank flipped it open and he and the President looked at

it. Mark had spent a lot of thought, and every spare minute of a trip Stateside, to come up with it. Nothing fancy for a woman like Emily Beale, but it had to be special. A band of black gold to symbolize the Night Stalkers, with a blue diamond the color of the Night Stalkers service patch. It was also the color of her eyes, but he figured that part of it was for him.

"Nice," the President whispered softly. "Really, Mark. That's perfect."

"Thank you, sir."

Frank closed the box and offered him a single solemn nod. Maybe there was a reason Frank was his best man. Mark now felt as if maybe, just maybe, he could do this.

"Music!" Mark felt like an idiot.

"What about it?" Frank frowned at him.

"Some best man you are. There isn't any! Shit! Emily deserves music. We've got to—"

"Too late," Frank nodded up toward the top of the green-grass aisle.

Standing at the very crest of the berm was a man in dress blues holding a rifle across his chest at Port Arms. His beret shone the bright red of Army Airborne beneath the brilliant afternoon sun.

Great, now *Emily* had someone who was going to shoot him if he messed up. Would that be before or after Frank kicked his ass?

10

——————

EMILY COULDN'T BELIEVE THAT COLONEL MICHAEL GIBSON, Delta Force's top field soldier, had flown in from some unnamed location just for her. She'd sent him an invitation, of course, but never expected him to come.

He had arrived as quietly as he always did—one moment no idea he was coming and the next there he was, standing at attention outside her bedroom door. He wore a full dress uniform—unheard of for a Delta operator—with his long hair tucked up in a red beret. Michael even had an HK416 combat rifle resting butt on the hardwood floor in the Order Arms position of full attention. No ceremonial M1 Garand of an honor guard. He bore a weapon of war, clearly declaring what he was willing to do in her defense.

"Privileged to be your honor guard, Major Beale," he greeted her formally when her mother opened the bedroom door to head to the wedding.

The tears—she hated crying—that had been hovering as she spent "girl time" with her mother (perhaps their first ever), almost spilled over, but she kept them back. Though she hugged Michael hard. He was living proof that she wasn't somehow dreaming her life; she really was a serving officer for the Night Stalkers.

He in turn had held her close as long as she'd needed him to, another unexpected gift.

Then he led the way through the house, out the door, and up to the lake, because of course a Delta Force colonel had already scouted the lay of the land with no one the wiser.

His wholly uncharacteristic short bark of laughter was all the warning she had before cresting the berm.

Emily didn't know whether to laugh or cry when she saw that every flier of the 5th Battalion D Company stood at full attention—all in their dress uniforms.

And all on the bride's side of the setting.

"Now those are some fine looking men," her mother whispered from her elbow as her father approached them. "And here's the handsomest of them all."

Emily had never thought of her father as handsome or not, but she was touched to see the happy misting in her mother's eyes after more than thirty years of marriage.

With Michael and her mother leading the way, and her father's arm for support, Emily finally found her balance.

She'd been second guessing her mother's advice all afternoon. She should be in uniform, like all of her teammates, but her mother had insisted this was a woman's day. And because her mother anticipated everything, and the two of them were the same dress size, Emily had finally caved in.

Taking a deep breath, she focused on Mark who looked impossibly strong and solid as he waited for her, and she concentrated on putting one foot in front of the other.

11

MARK DIDN'T EVEN BOTHER WONDERING WHERE MICHAEL HAD come from, it was just another tally for Emily in this lopsided wedding.

When Michael was about halfway down the slope to where he, Frank, and the President waited on the platform, Mark could finally see past him and Emily's mother.

The President's quiet, "Oh my goodness!" was far more than he could manage. His response might have been a gasp of amazement, if he'd still had the ability to breathe.

Emily wasn't wearing dress blues as he'd expected. Her mother had worn a soft green dress that practically blended her into the background of the outdoors and all the military uniforms. But not her daughter.

His Emily shimmered in a pale blue satin, off-the-shoulder, sheath dress. It revealed that the woman wearing it was both powerful and beautiful. Her blonde hair was braided on top of her head emphasizing her fantastic neck.

No adornment. No necklace. The only strong color was a flash of dark blue and silver on the upper left sleeve. Too bad everyone was standing at attention on the right side, they wouldn't get the joke as she passed by.

What kind of woman wore a Night Stalkers unit insignia on a high fashion wedding dress?

She beamed at him all the way down the aisle.

His kind of woman. Emily Beale.

12

———

EMILY HOPED THAT SOMEONE WAS TAPING THIS, BECAUSE SHE wasn't going to remember a single thing except for the way Mark looked at her.

She was floating lighter than when returning from a long mission just as the dawn light presaged the day. She was going to marry the man who would stay beside her through the years. The man she'd grow old with.

The man she'd have children with.

That thought had her catching her breath. For some reason, she'd never really thought about having children. But now she could feel it inside her as if it was already real. Not yet. There was still too much flying to be done. But someday. A son. Or perhaps a couple of girls. It wouldn't matter as long as the children were Mark's. She'd be more than content, so much more.

She could feel the warm tears sliding down her cheeks, but couldn't even raise a hand from clutching her bouquet of wild columbine to dab at them.

Then she heard a strange pause and began listening to Peter's rendition of the wedding ceremony.

"If any of you can show just cause why they may not lawfully be married, speak now; or else forever hold your peace," he prompted the crowd.

She'd given no thought to writing her own ceremony, her gift wasn't with words. *The Book of Common Prayer* had served couples for four hundred years, she saw no point in changing a single syllable.

There was a respectful silence.

Then Peter spoke up, "I don't know, *Squirt*. Are you sure this sad sack is up to your standards? After all, I heard about the whole cow-and-stream thing. Doesn't sound like a very brave..."

Emily moved fast. She was a little limited by the gown, but not enough to worry her.

She grabbed the book from his hands, then pushed sharply against the center of his chest.

Peter stumbled back one step.

Two.

There was no third step. The President of the United States, in one of his fine three-piece suits, fell off the edge of the platform and tumbled backward into the lake.

She managed to dodge clear of the spray, but Mark was soaked all down one side, receiving the main shot of water.

"Not again!" Mark groaned as he attempted to brush the water off his uniform.

"What the hell, Squirt!" Peter never swore, but standing chest deep in the pond was apparently enough to prompt him.

"It was inevitable, *Sneaker Boy.*"

Peter turned to Frank. "I thought you were supposed to protect me."

"I'll take a bullet for you, sir. But that was just plain dumb, Mr. President."

"At least you could help me out of here. I think I just lost a shoe in the mud."

"But you're all wet, sir." Frank, too, had been fast enough to dodge the worst of it.

Mark just waved him to wade around the platform to the shore.

She handed the book to Michael. "If you would be so kind?"

"Will it be legal?"

"He can sign the official certificate later." She waved a dismissive hand at Peter as he slogged ashore and sat on one of the many empty chairs on the groom's side. He had indeed lost a shoe, which was even better than merely dumping him in the Lincoln Memorial Reflecting Pool and soaking his new sneakers. "After *Shoe Boy* dries off."

Michael was, of course, magnificent as the officiate for the rest of the ceremony.

Mark's ring stole her breath away. He wasn't just marrying her, he was marrying the Night Stalker in her as well. He'd even thought to purchase a matching simple band of black gold in his own size. If she could have loved him more in that moment, she would have.

"By the power vested in President Peter Matthews," Michael concluded. "I now pronounce that you be man and wife together."

And Mark's kiss—albeit with a hug from just one side—brought all the sizzle a woman could hope for. It was a sizzle that promised to last a lifetime and she knew that Mark always, *always* delivered on his promises.

The 5th Battalion D Company roared out three cheers louder than all guns blazing.

She might be the only woman in the Night Stalkers, but that wouldn't always be the case. Until that day she knew one thing for certain, male or female, she truly belonged.

Mark's whispered, "Thank you for marrying me," as he held her, told her that she belonged for life.

KEE'S WEDDING

ABOUT THIS STORY

BEFORE THE END OF NIGHT STALKERS #2, I OWN THE DAWN...
Sniper Kee Smith knew two things for certain:

1. *she'd never be a mother*
2. *she'd never be a bride*

Wounded in battle, Captain Archie Stevenson will never fly again. He knows that he can't ask the woman and the war orphan they both love to take on such a burden.

Kee and Archie have fought many battles together, but can they face the hard truths and reach the altar for Kee's Wedding.

INTRODUCTION

KEE IS ELEMENTAL. SHE'S A FORCE OF NATURE IN EVERY WAY that I could think to make her one. Frankly, to a rather meek introvert like myself? She's terrifying!

I've been flattened by women like Kee in the past, because they didn't have her generous heart. No matter how much she refuses to acknowledge it, she can't get away from it and that's what I love about her.

The surprise for me is Dilya. In many ways, this is her story, especially once you reach the bonus scene. Dilya holds a unique place in my real-life world, one that I didn't realize until my wife pointed it out years after I'd written the original novel and this story.

I got my kid pre-packaged at six. Not a war orphan, but I fell for and married a single mother. When I finally met her kid, that was it. The connection ran as deep then as it still does decades later. I've been blessed with my family in ways I never imagined possible. Dilya is my tribute to the amazing person who changed my life that day...without me even realizing it.

1

———

"WHAT IF I'M NOT READY?"

"Since when haven't you been ready for anything?"

"This is different!" Kee Smith shouted her protest over the DAP Hawk helicopter's intercom.

Major Emily Beale did one of her magic tricks, slewing the helo around in a way that no other pilot possibly could. It gave Kee—perched at the side-gunner crew chief's position, close behind the copilot's seat—a clear shot on the lead vehicle in the column racing across the nighttime Afghan desert.

Kee grabbed the double handles on her M134 minigun, slid it out the window to the limit of the stops, and pulled the trigger. In answer, the electric motor spun the six-barrel Gatling gun up to five hundred rpm. The stream of 7.62mm ammunition raced out of the case, through the delinker, and into each barrel's chamber at precisely the right moment. She sent three thousand rounds per minute raking down out of the darkness. Every tenth round was an infrared tracer, brilliant green in her own night-vision gear—yet effectively invisible to anyone not so equipped.

Her first rounds struck less than ten meters in front of the lead vehicle, so she held steady and let the lead vehicle drive right into the hail of bullets. *Su-weet!* A practiced shake allowed her to destroy the engine. The truck lurched sideways off the road and slammed to a halt in the deep sand.

The copilot fired a Hydra 70 rocket to take out the anti-aircraft gun mounted on the truck bed as Kee continued to slice up the line of vehicles. Two RPGs were fired upwards, but in no particular direction and were no threat to their flight of four blacked-out helicopters. The Night Stalkers of the US Army's 160th SOAR ruled the night.

A Little Bird flying close beneath them took out the beater Toyota Corolla that had been the source of the RPGs as Kee and her fellow gunner Big John kept the convoy trapped on the road and behind the now-burning lead vehicle.

Big John was wisely staying out of this conversation. But if he so much as laughed, he'd be dead meat the moment they were back on the ground. She'd pulverize him herself, even if he was twice her size.

"I am so-o-o not ready for this shit!" Kee unleashed another chain of destruction on a captured Humvee. She must have managed to punch into some ammo cache through the turret gunner's position as the vehicle flared brightly inside, then exploded violently as they flew over it and raced once more into the desert.

"If I can do it, so can you," Emily replied with no real hint of sympathy as she rolled the Black Hawk completely over and somehow managed to come out of the maneuver headed back toward the column.

"But you're the legendary Major Emily Beale. I'm just

Sergeant Kee Smith. I'm not even that—I made up my last name."

"Get your act together, Kee," Major Beale sighed. "Night Stalkers Don't Quit!"

Having the motto of the 160th SOAR thrown in her face wasn't helping one bit. As to getting her shit together...since when was that even a possibility.

Emily certainly had though. She and Major Henderson had been married six months and still they walked about as if on some freaking honeymoon.

The MH-60M DAP Hawk banked hard, giving Kee a straight-down view on the militia's column. She unleashed more mayhem on them with her minigun.

This she could handle.

Her own wedding to Archie? In less than seventy-two hours? Not so much.

2

Captain Archibald Stevenson III, lay on the Italian beach and wondered how this had come to be his world. More accurately, he lay *in* the beach. His soon-to-be-adopted daughter, Dilya, had spent the last hour steadily covering him with a thick layer of sand until it lay on his chest like a lead blanket. It had been scorching hot at first with the Mediterranean sun beating down on him. Now that he was deeper under the sand there was a pleasant coolness to it.

Thankfully, pre-burial, he had pulled his hat low against the mid-morning sun. Dilya had made him promise not to peek, but he'd squinted out at her a few times anyway to make sure she was okay.

The eleven- or twelve-year-old Uzbekistani orphan—even she wasn't sure—appeared completely content as she worked some artistic magic with a bright blue plastic shovel the size of his palm. Kee had rescued the starving waif from a frigid mountaintop deep in a war zone barely three months ago. Now, in just three more days when he married

Kee, the three of them would become the most unlikely family imaginable.

Despite her constantly prodigious appetite, Dilya was still pencil thin, though no longer gaunt. She'd been little more than a ragged ghost at first—and as flighty as one, disappearing at the least alarm. She'd settled into herself in surprising ways and proven herself highly adaptable. First at Forward Operating Base Bati where he and Kee had been stationed, then back in the States with him and his parents after he'd been shot and had to have his shoulder replaced.

The two of them had seen Kee only briefly during these last three months, but the transformation between them had been nothing short of miraculous. Archie loved Dilya, with her long, dark hair and mystical green eyes, and had no doubt that she loved him back. But the connection between Dilya and Kee was closer than he'd ever imagined a mother and daughter could be—though one was born of Uzbek refugees and the other on the streets of East L.A.

Kee.

Archie resisted the urge to itch at the sand which had now penetrated every single pore. Dilya had been very exasperated at the damage to her artwork when he'd done so earlier. He tried focusing on the soft lapping of the Mediterranean waves, the soft lilt of Italian among other families enjoying the sunny morning, even the laughter of their children—but all he could think about was the itchy sand.

Kee was an even bigger puzzle than Dilya. How had she slipped into his heart so completely? She was feisty, obnoxious, tough-as-nails, and an amazing soldier. Her permanently dark tan skin, Asian narrow eyes, and exceptionally curved body had made her a fantasy to look at. Even her dark hair with its saucy little blonde-dyed strip had been cute as hell.

There was a dark side to her as well, that she'd revealed to him in her typical manner—a single, massive emotional blast. One moment she'd been this sexy companion who he couldn't get enough of, and the next she'd been the miracle proof of what could be done by pure willpower. Everything about her had a deeper meaning, even the little stripe of golden hair.

There had never been a woman like her!

Whenever they were apart, he wondered how he could be with someone from such a different world. His parents were upper crust Boston and Mom was a top strategic consultant to the White House on global geopolitics. He himself was a top ten West Point grad. Kee had finished high school by getting her GED before becoming an Army infantry grunt and working her way up to being a Night Stalker.

There was no way the three of them should work well as a unit.

Yet whenever they were together, his mismatched family-to-be made absolute perfect sense. Kee was so damned...alive! It made him wonder what she saw in him. Not that he was complaining, but it made him wonder.

"Soon, Dilya. Soon we will all be back together."

The slight girl barely nodded as she focused on her sandy creation. Then she glanced at his face. "I say no peekings. *Ha?*" *Yes?* in Uzbek.

"No peekings. *Ha.*" He didn't bother to correct her *peekings* and simply closed his eyes once more. Her English was improving fantastically—with the help of nightly doses of *Winnie the Pooh* or *Charlotte's Web*—far faster than he'd ever done with a foreign tongue, but she must be sick of the constant little corrections. Time to give the kid a break.

Archie wasn't sure which of them he was reassuring anyway. The doctors had signed off on his recovery. His shoulder was as good as new—almost. He'd never be able to fly to 160th SOAR standards again, but that was the only real limitation.

But without flying, his future was a complete unknown. Too many options.

His mother wanted him to return to D.C. and work with her consulting firm. She'd spent much of last night working to convince him she was right, and almost had.

The Army wanted to slot him into mission planning at the Pentagon.

Or maybe he needed to break away. Be out on his own, doing who knew what.

But he wasn't on his own.

He'd promised that in three days he'd be saying *yes* to being a family. A family was meant to be together, not scattered across the planet. For three months he'd sought an answer, but been stumped every time.

If he couldn't fly... But no answer lay on the other side of that question.

Soon they'd be back together, he'd reassured Dilya.

But would they? He'd met Kee on her first day with the Night Stalkers just four months ago. She'd barely started in this phase of her military career when his future with the Night Stalkers had been taken away by a gunshot wound. There was no future for them. Getting married made no sense whatso—

"You look now."

"You *can* look now," then he bit his tongue. So much for giving Dilya a language break.

"You *can* look now. You can *look* now. You can look..." Dilya whispered variations to herself as she integrated the correction into her understanding of English.

And what would part of being a fractured family would be good for her?

Maybe he should walk away while he still could.

Do what was right for them.

He opened his eyes and squinted against the brightness. His parents, who had picked up the burden of caring for him and Dilya these last months, had flown out for the wedding last night. They'd been sleeping in, so he'd left a note where they could find him and Dilya on the beach. Now they were standing by his feet and looking down at him with slightly confused smiles. They often didn't understand Dilya's curiously mashed-up view of her past culture colliding with her new exposure to America, but loved her like a grandchild nonetheless. Kee they were far less sure about.

Archie tipped his head up to try and see, but the sand covering his body all of the way to his neck stopped him. So much sand that he couldn't sit up really. He pushed a little harder, but his new shoulder twinged and he dropped back down to rest his head on the beach. Three months to full range of motion, but another six months or more until it would be back up to full strength. Light duty only.

Dilya looked panicked, turning between him and her sand creation, only now understanding that he was in no position to see what she had spent most of the morning building.

Taking pity on him, Dad snapped a photo with his phone and then came to hold it where Archie could see it.

Archie saw what it was right away.

Laying on her side atop his chest, was a half-size version

of Kee. And curled in her arms was a half-Dilya-sized figure. A pair of powerful arms made of sand sprouted from where his shoulders were buried beneath the sand. They cradled both the woman and girl lying upon his chest.

Archie had always seen Kee as the anchor of their new family because she was such a force of nature.

But that's not how Dilya saw it.

She saw him.

"Oh, Dilya."

Her expression was carefully devoid of emotion. But he could see the sunlight catching the watery brightness in her green eyes. A girl who had lost so much looked at him—at *him*—with tears of hope. How could he deny that?

"*Ha.* Dilya. Very *ha.*"

3

"Not gonna be catching this boy doing anything that kind of crazy," Big John declared as he thumped his dinner tray on the mess tent's table.

The place was buzzing after last night's successful attack. It jazzed up the whole camp, even the people who hadn't been along for the ride. The small team of Delta Force operators were quiet in their corner, of course, but the 75th Rangers were talking it up as if it had been their own mission.

Majors Beale and Henderson were doing their usual table-for-two off to one side so as not to impose their command presence on the rest of the team's celebratory mood.

"Doing what kind of crazy?" Kee asked because it was expected, but kept an eye on the majors. She'd tried picturing herself in their shoes: she and Archie. Content to simply sit together over a meal. But she could never make it happen in her head. The majors were the perfect couple. The two most decorated Night Stalker pilots in any battalion. Both beautiful, Mark poster-boy handsome and

Emily magazine-ad blonde. Both so assured of their place in the world.

That could never be her.

Then she spotted that Emily had a single foot forward under the table, the sole of her boot resting on the toe of Henderson's. It made them human and *that* she could almost imagine...just not for someone like her.

"That's some crazy-ass shit you're gonna be doing," John was digging into a massive serving of pasta slathered with red sauce, pesto, and a fistful of Parmesan.

"It's me," she turned her attention back to her own meal. "Crazy shit is what I do. What are you talking about this time?" She spun a forkful of spaghetti and stuffed it in her mouth.

"'Bout you getting married, Smith."

Kee almost choked.

"That's way the hell outside the mission profile," Crazy Tim agreed as he dropped into the seat across from her, then reached across and stole a slice of garlic bread even though he had several of his own.

She casually reached over and took his apple pie before "accidentally" dumping his glass of milk in the tray.

Tim didn't even blink as he fished his fork out of the white puddle swirling around the bottom of his plate, licked it off, and began eating. He ignored the milk pool as if it was just a decoration.

"We like Archie and all, but marriage?" Tim mumbled around a big bite of Kee's stolen garlic bread. "Seriously, Smith, what's up with that? Is that how someone gets a woman to say *I do*? Gets his shoulder shot up and you go all swoony for him?"

Big John clasped his huge hands together, tucked them under his chin, and fluttered his eyelashes at her. Six-four of towering black man swooning like a little girl was too much and actually earned him a laugh. For a reward she gave him Tim's slice of apple pie. She desperately needed to laugh.

When it was someone like Archie, who had kept fighting beside her until the mission was complete *after* having his shoulder shot up, it definitely did count. When he played so sweetly with Dilya, or called Kee herself "Helen of Troy" for being sexy enough to launch a thousand ships, that counted to.

The rest of the crew from the majors' two DAP Hawks landed farther down the table, but they were much more concerned with reliving the mission, so she ignored them. Connie, the quiet new mechanic, veered aside and sat off at a table by herself. She was turning out to be an okay person, but Kee didn't have time to think about her at the moment. Maybe after Kee was back from her honeymoon.

Her *honeymoon?*

Shit! Since when was she the sort of person that would ever have one of those?

"Just between two gunners," Big John leaned down and whispered softly while Tim was busy trying to steal Dusty's soda to replace his own spilled milk, "I think Archie is one of the luckiest shits anywhere, Kee. You're hot as they get and you totally kick ass."

Kee could only stare at him in surprise. Four months ago he'd been pissed as hell that Tim, his best friend who he'd flown with for a decade, had been bumped over to Henderson's helo to make room for her. She'd also been a baby Night Stalker fresh out of training.

She now had a place aboard a DAP Hawk, the respect of her teammates, and Archie and Dilya waiting for her. Didn't mean there wasn't more to prove...

But John nodded that he meant it. Wild!

Dusty fended off Tim with enough force to flip his chair over, with Tim still in it.

Kee and Big John lifted their trays off the table just in time; in Tim's backward flail, he kicked the bottom of the table. Curses sounded all down the length of it as glasses and sodas toppled.

The two of them set their trays back down.

"Uh, thanks," was all she could think to say.

"Nothing but the truth," John nodded as he returned to eating.

"What's the truth?" Tim righted his chair and thumped his butt back into it.

"That you aren't worth the trouble of even knowing, shithead," John rumbled out.

"Hey, somebody's got to keep things lively," then, as if nothing had happened, Tim grinned and continued eating Kee's slice of garlic bread that had started the whole hoopla.

4

_____

"IT WILL BE OKAY," THOUGH ARCHIE WASN'T SURE WHICH OF them he was reassuring. He and Dilya stood on the tarmac outside Hangar Four on the military side of Pisa's Galileo Galilei Airport. She held his hand tightly.

It had been two months since they'd seen Kee in person. She'd managed a few video calls, but Dilya didn't seem to understand those. What if they'd grown distant?

Dilya had built her sand sculpture around some image of Kee the mother figure. Kee was many things, but that wasn't one of them. She was tender with Dilya, but he wouldn't describe her as maternal.

Tugging his hand, Dilya pointed suddenly at the sky.

Archie squinted up at the plane and waited for it to resolve from being a tiny black dot coming toward the runway. Four-engine turboprop. Hercules C-130. He squeezed her hand, hoping that this was it.

Dilya squared her shoulders and checked her clothes. She had adopted portions of American teen style, but made it her own. Her Muslim heritage had stuck in her modesty, and he could only hope that lasted. Leggings under khaki shorts. A loose blouse that hid her pre-teen curves and a stone-washed denim jacket despite the September warmth. A trio of light scarves braided into a multi-colored neon twist meant this was her fancy wear for special occasions—at least that's how he was interpreting it.

He'd put on tan khakis and a black t-shirt without thinking about it—standard off-duty wear. Except he was *way* off duty.

There was a bright screech of tires as the plane touched down, followed immediately by the heavy roar of the four eight-bladed propellers reversing hard to dump speed. His nerves were climbing irrationally but he couldn't stop them.

"I'd rather be facing a ZU-23," a particularly lethal Russian-made anti-aircraft gun.

Dilya looked up at him strangely.

"Never mind." Some things were unexplainable, even if she was getting the language. He concentrated on keeping his grasp on her hand light and calm.

The big plane rolled up, shut down, then lowered its rear ramp.

"Hey, Arch!" Big John strode down the ramp and came over to lock him in a bear hug while Tim thumped him hard on the back. Major Henderson strolled up and shook his hand hard enough that Archie could only hope that the doctors had reattached his shoulder as solidly as they said they had.

Emily walked up to him. Ten years they'd flown together. Ever since she'd picked him out of the crowd at West Point in a History of the Military Art course, they'd served side by side. She was so far out of his league, that there had never been anything between them. Or maybe the spark had simply never been there in the first place.

She reached out and rested her hand as lightly as a feather on his shoulder before looking directly at him.

He nodded. Yes, it was all okay, even if he could never fly beside her again.

Emily squeezed his shoulder lightly in acknowledgement. Between them there was no need for words.

Then, unexpectedly, she shifted her hand to his cheek and offered him a nod. "It's all good, Archie."

He tried to see what she meant, but couldn't read the expression on her face. Finally, Emily offered one of her fleeting, all-knowing smiles. Then she nodded behind herself, where she couldn't possibly see what was happening.

There, kneeling at the foot of the ramp, was the most amazing woman he'd ever met. Her arms were filled with Dilya who had a throttle-hold around Kee's neck.

But even as her hands were reassuring the little girl, her dark eyes were watching him.

Archie didn't even remember walking away from Emily and crossing to her. It was a short distance, one measured in barely noticed handshakes and hearty congratulations.

Two months since he'd seen her and Kee looked even more incredible than he'd remembered. Barely five-six, powerful curves, soldier strong, dark brown hair that fell straight to her jawline, and her trademark thin strip of golden blond. Her dark past was always with her.

She rose to her feet, holding Dilya lightly in her arms.

She didn't open one arm to greet him in—it wasn't her way. Didn't even smile which was a little odd.

But when he wrapped his arms around both of them, she did bury her face against his new shoulder and breathe him in.

He kissed them both on top of the head and then prayed that he wouldn't screw this up.

5

_____

"WHAT DO YOU THINK?" KEE DID A LITTLE DANCE IN FRONT OF the mirror. At the moment, she, Dilya, Emily, and Archie's mom, Betty, had command of the little wedding dress shop. Outside the window, Italy was bustling by and she couldn't wait to get out into the sunshine and play.

The dress landed dangerously high on the thigh—no sitting down in this one. The cleavage had been designed with someone like her in mind. Wedding lace of the purest white made her tan-dark skin stand out and the racing-strip red trim just screamed wild and sexy.

"This will just kill Archie. I know it will."

A quick spin as she watched in the mirror convinced her of its awesomeness for liquifying men's brains on first sight.

"Seriously, could it be any better?" She spun once more and stopped facing Dilya.

Dilya sat in the pink-and-white armchair with her head down on the knees she was pulling tight against her chest. The other arm was over the top of her head as if to make sure she didn't accidentally look up.

"C'mon, kid. A little skin isn't going to burn out your eyes."

"What means burn out—" Dilya started to look up, saw Kee, yelped, and ducked her head back down.

Kee looked at the ceiling and sighed. "This isn't happening."

She looked helplessly over at the shop clerk who merely shrugged. Wedding dresses weren't a big stock item at a forward operating base in a dark corner of northern Pakistan, so she'd had to wait for Italy to buy one.

Archie and the boys had been shooed off to Vernazza (about an hour train ride up the coast) for a bachelor's party —or at least to visit a good *taverna*. Vernazza had been one of their favorite towns when they visited here before the fateful mission that had wounded Archie. It also had a harbor deep enough for the sailboat they'd be honeymooning on so that they could leave directly from the ceremony.

He'd looked an absolute wreck—a gorgeous one, but a wreck. His wavy brown hair had been lightened by the sun and his tan had been darkened, making him even more impossibly handsome. But it was his eyes that had gotten to her. She'd felt consumed by his wide, sky-blue eyes.

All through lunch he hadn't stopped staring at her, and wouldn't let go of her hand. He was being a little intense for her and it was kind of freaking her out. On the other hand, she'd missed him the moment he'd left for the train. Kee did her best to ignore that fact because it didn't sound at all like her.

Meanwhile, the women had stayed in Pisa to do a little shopping, especially dress shopping.

"Oh my," Betty looked Kee up and down as she came out of the racks, carrying a pretty Italian sundress covered with stylized sweet pea blossoms that would look great on such an elegant woman. "Well, that will surely get Archie's attention. Although, I'm not sure if he'll be able to say his vows if you are wearing that."

"That's what I like about it."

Emily peeked over the barrier of one of the changing rooms. Kee could see the smile reach Emily's eyes, though she didn't say a word.

"Dilya doesn't approve."

The girl just squeaked, but didn't raise her head.

"She may have a point," Emily stepped through the swinging door that had masked her from eyes to knees. She looked amazing. Her slender form was perfectly outlined in a clinging sheath dress that was the same light topaz blue as her eyes.

"Well, if I had a figure like yours, I'd steal that dress right off your back. How is someone who looks like me supposed to look that beautiful? Skin is reliable—works every time."

Emily, Betty, and the shop clerk began running her through different dresses. Kee didn't let them take away the hot little number, though they tried several times.

By dress six—or maybe it was sixteen—her patience was wearing thin. Didn't Italian women have breasts? They must all be as slender as the major or as elegant as Archie's mom. The wedding dresses that were built for women with a full figure assumed they were far taller than she was. Or didn't have hips to match. Or had the breasts and hips, but also the waist to go with them.

There was no time for alterations. Most of the team was on a three-day pass: a day to get here, the ceremony tomorrow, and a day to get back. She was pretty touched at how many of them had come. The only one missing was—

"Hey, where's Connie? Did anyone think to invite her?"

Emily nodded. "She didn't want to intrude."

Huh! Not the cold bitch that Kee had first assumed—nor the chill soldier either. Hadn't guessed at her being sensitive. Being shy wasn't something Kee had a lot of experience with, but that would explain a lot. Made her actually like the woman. Definitely had to check her out more after the honeymoon.

"Well, I'm pretty much sunk here. Dilya will just have to suck it up and—"

But when she turned for the changing room, a dress hung on the door. It was really pretty, with a high neck, half sleeves, and a long skirt made of a few overlapping layers of lace beneath a sheer.

Emily stepped up beside her and after a long moment's inspection made a considering "Hmmm" sound. Betty and the shop clerk were still rummaging through the racks.

Dilya was back in her armchair watching Kee intently.

6

A CHEER ROARED THROUGH THE SPORTS BAR AS A TELEVISION showed the Italian soccer team scoring, then heartrending groans as a ref signaled a disallowed goal, made the sign for pushing, and tossed the ball to the French goalie to bring it back into play.

Archie leaned against the wall behind his chair. They'd shoved him into the back of the corner table then sandwiched him in to either side. Major Henderson, Big John, Tim, Dusty, Captain Richardson, and some of the Little Bird pilots as well.

Perhaps they were being friendly. Or perhaps they understood just how close he was to hitting the ground running and not stopping until he hit Kansas.

He let the conversation drift back and forth, mostly without him, only dipping into the air turbulence of the talk when he couldn't avoid it.

Somehow they'd found a sports bar in Italy that was both Italian and so very not. Big screen TVs were mounted all around a room that had been built of stone around the time of Charlemagne, or maybe Caesar. But rather than the

American fare of baseball, football, and boxing, they were serving out soccer, Formula 1 auto racing, and cricket. The bar was lined with taps that read: Peroni, Heineken Italia, Menabrea, Tarricone, and other beers he'd never heard of. There was a domed, wood-fired pizza oven, covered in black-and-white tiles patterned like a soccer ball.

There were other differences from American bars as well. Far more couples than single men, and kids too. And as often as not when there was a baby or toddler, it was the father tending to it rather than the mom. There was a lively, happy buzz, all of it in flowing Italian that sounded almost as beautiful as Spanish.

"Scares you spitless, doesn't it?" Mark boomed out cheerfully from one side. To his other side, Big John had a liter glass wrapped in one of his big hands. Tim had dragged the others up to the bar where he was calling play by play on a rugby game that he clearly didn't understand. The Italians at the bar were joining in the spirit of it and misdirecting him at every chance.

Archie weighed the odds of getting past Mark or Big John and decided that his chances were too slim.

Unable to speak, he could only nod.

Mark answered his nod sagely, still wearing his mirrored shades despite the bar's dim interior. "Know the feeling. The day I stood at the head of that aisle with Emily walking toward me? That's the day they should have awarded me the Medal of Honor for bravery far exceeding the call of duty."

"Don't sound so scary to me," Big John knocked back a large swallow of beer.

"Just wait until it's your turn," Mark scoffed. "How about that cute new girl on your team? What's her name? Connie something?"

John flinched badly enough to shake the table.

Archie didn't know who they were talking about. It felt strange to not know something about the company. As if he belonged even less than he'd thought he did, which wasn't much any more.

"Not a chance. That woman is enough to drive a dude batshit."

"Willing to bet a twenty on that?" Mark slapped a twenty-euro note on the table.

"No way, asshole," John was shaking his head. "Makes me ill just thinking about it."

"That's Major Asshole to you," Mark tried pushing his twenty across, but John wasn't taking it.

"No argument from me on that one, boss." John glared down at his beer.

Archie was fine with the conversation moving on without him. Maybe he could just fade away. Dilya seemed to do that sometimes, just suddenly—not be there. It was scary as hell when she did it unexpectedly. She'd even managed to slip aboard a black ops mission with them once with no one the wiser until it was too late to turn back. Turned out in the end that it was a good thing she had.

"You know..." John cricked his neck. "Don't know if I should be saying this, but your bride is kinda wound up about this as well."

"Kee?" Archie shook his head. "No, John. You're reading that wrong. Kee always has her act together. Knows exactly what she wants."

"Willing to bet a twenty on that?" Mark tried shoving the bill in his direction.

"Don't, Archie," Big John warned. "That's a sure loss. Chick is freakin'."

"But if she doesn't want to marry me then..." Archie

tapered off as John seemed to grow twice his already substantial size.

"I didn't say that. Just said she was freaking. Time to man up, dude. You don't put a ring on that gal's finger tomorrow, you aren't gonna be nothing but a bloody smear on the sidewalk. Don't care what your rank is, sir. This is man to man."

Archie studied his beer. It sounded as if Kee wanted out.

Or maybe not. She was here in Italy and out buying a dress. By nightfall, they'd be in the same hotel room. All through lunch he'd kept looking at her in surprise, trying to figure out how he could be lucky enough to marry her.

And there was no questioning the way that she'd held Dilya when she stepped off the plane.

And no questioning the way she'd let him hold the two of them. Just as Dilya had carved it in the sand. And when he'd seen the photo, he remembered how he'd felt, as if his heart couldn't get any fuller.

Time to man up, dude. Good advice.

"Still a got a twenty on you and Connie, John," Mark's expression was inscrutable behind his mirrored shades. "What do you say? Want some easy money?"

Big John snarled, hauled out his wallet and slapped a pair of twenties on the table. "I'll take that bet twice. Double no-way no-how."

Henderson nodded happily and refreshed all of their glasses from the pitcher.

KEE LAY AWAKE ON THE BIG BED.

Vernazza wasn't that big a town. A small harbor, mostly filled with fishing skiffs behind a long breakwater. Behind the seawall, it was really just a single circle street with a lot of small branches to the sides. Tucked up against the cliffs of Liguria, it was one of the five towns that made up Cinque Terre.

So after arriving on the train and leaving their new dresses at the hotel, they had gone out for their own small gal celebration. Gelato then a sausage and pepper calzone—in that order. Pear gelato was in season and it wasn't worth missing it. She and Dilya had split a second one after dinner, though Emily and Betty had declared one was sufficient.

They'd seen the bar where the men had ended up—it wasn't hard to find as it had the rowdiest crowd anywhere in the tiny town. They'd stood outside in the falling darkness and looked in through the window. Archie and Tim facing off against a pair of Italian men at a foosball table with a big crowd gathered around them. Archie looked a little manic—cheering his own team, gasping in despair at each loss, and crowing with each victory.

It wasn't like him, and Kee still lay awake contemplating the meaning of it all.

Dilya, originally set to sleep on the couch in their room, had slipped into bed with her and Kee had let her. Her nerves were calmer when the girl was with her. Everything somehow made sense—which was ridiculous, because Kee was supposed to be dead.

She'd never expected to live this long—nearly hadn't twice and she had the scars to prove it. Yet against all odds, she had. Not just survived, but tomorrow would become both wife and adoptive mother. That wasn't on any life plan she'd ever had.

The door opened quietly.

Kee narrowed her eyes so that they wouldn't catch the nightlight she'd left on.

Archie peeked in. Not the wild man she'd barely recognized at the foosball table. Instead, it was the man she'd known from the first day. He stood just inside the door: shoes in his hand, silent, watching.

Considerate, thoughtful. That was Archie.

But he kept standing there. Looking down at her and Dilya as a smile slowly grew on his face. He'd looked so serious at the airport, which had completely unnerved her. But now—even in the dim light—she could see the lopsided smile that she so loved settle over him. That was the man she was marrying.

He watched them for a few moments before going over to the couch. It wasn't near long enough for a grown man, it was barely long enough for Dilya. But he didn't seem to mind. Instead, he simply curled up with that goofy smile on his face.

She fell asleep with him watching over his new family.

8

────────

ARCHIE WASN'T SURE IF HE'D EATEN DINNER, BUT HE'D SURELY drunk it. Attempting to sleep off the aftereffects—while twisted up like a pretzel on the short couch—hadn't worked.

Mark handed him several aspirin and a double espresso, then dug out his uniform and began ironing it for him. If there was one thing the Army taught you, it was how to have an immaculate uniform.

Kee and Dilya were gone of course.

He showered, dressed, and was fed more coffee before he truly regained consciousness. He came to stand at the altar.

"Hell of a setting you chose," Mark sounded pleased.

Archie could only squint against the brightness of the morning. They stood at the end of the tiny harbor's massive breakwater. To his back was a line of huge stones that were piled a story tall above the quiet Mediterranean. It was hard to believe that it served a purpose, yet he'd seen pictures of the winter storms blowing fifty feet of spray up against its stout bulwark.

In front of him Vernazza harbor stretched only a few

hundred feet from side to side. In the middle floated the thirty-foot sloop he'd rented in La Spezia and brought here two days ago. That was his honeymoon with Kee—sailing along the Ligurian and Amalfi coast while Dilya was off with his parents.

Instead of romantic, it now sounded sad. Part of their courtship had been aboard a sailboat, poking their way down this very coast. But picturing someone as vital as Kee with a husband as directionless as himself...not a good image.

Vernazza itself filled the cul-de-sac formed by the sea cliffs with four- and five-story buildings clustered so tightly together that it was hard to imagine there were cobbled streets winding among them—deep in shadow and spangled with surprising patches of sunlight. The buildings were the red and oranges of sunset, accented by the lone white bell tower of the Santa Margherita church. He could just make out the clock that said ten minutes to ten o'clock. Beyond the town, a steeply terraced vineyard masked any harsh stone with a bounty of grape vines.

At the far end of the breakwater, guarding the original entrance to the harbor against pirates before the breakwater had been built, Doria Castle commanded the town. It perched atop a high rocky bluff.

Vernazza was ancient. Solid. It dated back a thousand years and might be much unchanged for another thousand.

It made Archie feel unimportant, even ephemeral.

"I have no place here." He knew it. No place to serve. He was about to marry a woman he could no longer serve beside. What was he doing? It wasn't right. He should—

"Been meaning to talk to you about that," Mark was looking at him.

Archie could only look at the twin pretender version of

himself reflected back at him by the major's sunglasses. Even the uniform felt wrong. Archie had flown beside Emily for a decade since West Point and now he wore the dress uniform as if he somehow still belonged.

"You're back on the active duty?"

"Light duty," Archie grunted out. "They said it will be a year before I can fly again. You know as well as I do what that does to a flier's skills." It would take another year after that to get his skills back up to Night Stalker standards, if he even could.

Mark turned to track a pair of stunning brunettes in European-skimpy bikinis as they headed out to lie on the rocks and do a little sunbathing. They, in turn, definitely had eyes for the two men in full American military dress uniforms.

Archie was too tired to do more than notice them, despite their coy looks and increased hip sway.

"Been missing you in operations," Mark said without facing him.

"Great." He must be recovering from last night's excesses —definitely his most excessive ever—because he'd managed to rediscover sarcasm.

"Emily is the queen of tactical, but we never understood just how much you brought to the game strategically. You see the big picture far faster than anyone else in the entire company. If you hadn't been so powerful a team—the strategic and the tactical together—you'd have had your own bird a long time ago."

"Never cared about that. Not gonna happen now anyway, is it?" Archie tried to shake off being so morose. It was a more unfamiliar coat that the dress uniform he now wore. But the doubt still stuck to his shoulders.

Archie glanced at Mark, but he was walking away to

greet the Army Chaplin who had taken the train up from Camp Darby in Pisa. Probably hadn't even heard Archie's complaint.

Others began arriving. Tim and Big John weren't in formal blue mess dress uniforms, but were definitely cutting a swath in their Army service uniforms. Their passage along the breakwater had collected a small gaggle of tourist admirers, and a few locals as well. They each had an Italian beauty on their arm—ones Archie vaguely recalled from the bar last night.

There wasn't room for chairs or aisles, but there were two rises in the concrete backing for the breakwater that were soon filled as benches. He'd been thrilled that Mark and some of the other guys had come. He was an only child and Kee had no family at all, so it was nice to have the extra people. But as more gawkers drifted their way, it became clear that they were going to have a big wedding after all.

Big John came up and slapped his back with enough cheerful bonhomie to drive the last of Archie's hangover into the Vernazza harbor.

"Looking awesome, sir," Tim saluted him.

"Feeling like shit, Tim," Archie returned the gesture.

"No way," Big John grabbed him by the shoulder and shook him in a friendly fashion that almost took Archie's feet out from under him. "You can't be—not with what you're about to do. Remember what I said last night."

Archie looked down at the storm-weathered concrete and wondered if Big John really would deliver on his threat to squish him into it if he was dumb enough to not marry Kee. So, he changed the subject.

"I'm never, ever going drinking with you two again. And that's an order."

"Yes, sir!" Big John saluted this time.

"Sounds like a bet," Tim looked ready to rush off and find a six-pack in order to take up the challenge right then and there.

Archie went for another subject change, "Like the bet John made that he wasn't going to fall for Connie."

"Connie?" Tim turned on his friend utterly delighted. "You and the egghead mechanic? Dude, I didn't know. When's the wedding?"

"The twelfth of never," Big John grumbled.

"No, seriously. She's cute as hell. Weird in several ways, but majorly cute."

"Fine, you can have her," John was all magnanimity.

"Not if you already got a bet on."

"He bet me," Mark rejoined them, "that he *wasn't* going to fall for her."

"Oh!" Tim crowed. "This is gonna be so excellent!"

Tim and Big John began arguing about it in the way only best friends could.

The crowd was thickening. Soon, the entire breakwater would be crammed full.

Archie needed to talk to Kee, try to talk her out of it, before it was too late. But there was no way that he was going to get to talk to her before the ceremony.

The church tower clock read five minutes to ten. Five minutes to their agreed start time.

Could he do it at the altar?

Should he?

This couldn't be happening.

9

————

"THERE'S NO WAY I CAN DO THIS!" KEE LOOKED DOWN AT THE waterfront aghast.

A small cluster of men in full military uniforms stood at the end of the breakwater. Even at this distance, Archie and Mark stood out in their dress uniforms with wide red lapels, white shirt fronts, and blue pants with gold stripes on the side. Between her and the wedding party were hundreds of tourists. Everything from sundresses to jeans with bikini tops. Men, women, teens, baby strollers, octogenarians: an entire slice of Italian locals and tourists.

Emily offered one of her all-knowing smiles while Betty patted her arm consolingly.

Dilya clung to her hand.

The four of them had enjoyed a quiet breakfast of lattes and cornetto pastries, with Dilya drinking a cup of hot chocolate almost as big as her head.

"We'll just forge a path for you," Emily went to step out of the hotel entry overlooking the harbor. Kee grabbed her and pulled her back.

"It's not the people that are freaking me out."

Emily furrowed her brow at Kee. Betty was also looking confused.

"Look. For both of you marriage was a logical step."

"So not," Emily started. "I never—"

"But you did," Kee cut her off. "Your parents were married. Had a kid. Raised you. All of that. It's natural to you."

Kee managed to drag in a breath, but any calm that she needed just wasn't climbing aboard.

"I'm being serious here, I was born on the streets. Mom took care of me when she wasn't too stoned to remember who I was. Marriage was something the judge did for people who somehow thought they'd last more than a year or two together. I sure never did. I *can't* be someone's wife. I *can't* be someone's mother." She looked down at Dilya who was watching the whole tirade with worry, but probably didn't understand one word in ten.

Kee held up their joined hands to demonstrate. "This isn't me!"

For once Emily didn't have some simple answer. And that was even more scary, because Emily knew everything.

"I love Archie. I'm sure of that. But being a Wife and Mother, how am I supposed to do that? I don't even know what that means or what it's supposed to look like. I—"

Betty rested a hand on Kee's arm which felt as if it was all she that kept her from flying apart. "I wasn't a good mother."

"But," Kee waved her hand helplessly toward the waterfront, "Archie. He's such an amazing man. You did that."

Betty tipped her head for a moment. "You were the one who pointed that out to me, not many miles from here—back when we first met and I didn't know or trust you. I still find it to be a curious thought. Yes, I love my son and he *has* become an amazing man, *despite* my feeble attempts at bringing him up properly. I have given this a great deal of thought since then."

"Please tell me you learned something?" Kee peeked out the window at the still-growing crowd and shivered.

"I learned—"

Dilya tugged on Kee's arm, pulling until she had to kneel to face her.

"What?"

Dilya brushed her hands over Kee's hair, then her neck and shoulders as if trying to tell her something. Then, after a sigh, reached into a pocket of her dress and pulled out two squares of tightly folded cloth.

Kee recognized them right away. It was the two scarves they had bought together in a Pakastani market a lifetime ago. Kee had forgotten about them, but apparently Dilya hadn't.

She very carefully unfolded Kee's scarf. The edge trim of the green of new life surrounded a field of midnight blue filled with stars—a masterpiece of weaving craft. It had been her Night Stalker scarf.

Dilya folded it point to point then rolled it like a bandana. It wouldn't go with her hair and around her neck it would break the line of the wedding dress. But Kee decided it was best to keep her thoughts to herself.

She needn't have worried. Dilya wrapped it several times around Kee's wrist and tied the ends together making a Night Stalker bracelet of the beautiful cloth.

Kee took Dilya's far simpler scarf, a field of the same green with the dark blue for trim, and tied it over Dilya's hair as would be appropriately modest for her Muslim heritage. She took a moment to finger brush Dilya's thick hair back over her shoulders.

Then Dilya hugged her. Not the fierce hug of greeting at the airport that had almost choked out tears along with Kee's breath. Instead, it was simply a hug of childish love. Except there had never been anything childish about Dilya. Nothing in her hard past had allowed for something as simple as childhood. It was but one of the true bonds between them.

"That is what I learned," Betsy whispered quietly. "I can't picture myself being a good mother or a good wife. But I *can* picture a good mother or wife being me. Something in who I am made Archie. Not what I think I should have been, just in who I was. And who I am with his father, my husband. You will be an amazing mother and wife, Kee, because it is already in you."

Kee took Dilya's hand again as she rose back to her feet.

Emily wasn't looking at her, but rather down at Dilya in surprise. With a look that Kee now understood. For the first time, the daunting Major Emily Beale was also realizing that she could be a mother someday—without changing the magnificent woman she was.

"Magnificent woman," Kee said it softly. "Magnificent *women*," she declared with more certainty. "The four of us are magnificent, aren't we?"

Betty and then Emily nodded tentatively once. Then again with growing smiles.

"Let's do this."

And Dilya held her hand tightly as they stepped out of the hotel entry and onto the crowded street.

10

——————

ARCHIE LOOKED UP AS THE CHURCH BELL BEGAN STRIKING TEN o'clock. It echoed across the harbor and town so clearly that speech became difficult.

Then he spotted the women the instant they stepped out of the hotel door, though they were on the far side of the harbor.

"You ready, Archie?" Mark shouted above the bell as it switched from ringing the hour to playing some involved piece of music. He clamped a hand on Archie's shoulder as if to make sure he didn't simply dive into the harbor and swim for the sailboat...or maybe just straight out to sea.

"No!"

Mark started to laugh, but cut it off after he looked at Archie's face.

"So help me to god, Mark. How am I supposed to saddle Kee with a husband who can't even be with her? Who can no longer serve?" He flapped his arm and ignored the deep pinch. *Who isn't even a whole man?* "Being a pilot is all I ever was. And now I'm not even that."

"You wait until the bride is walking toward you to tell me

this shit?" Mark actually shoved his sunglasses up into his hair revealing his steel-gray eyes. He squinted for a long moment. "No... Tell me you aren't about to do something as stupid as I think you are."

Archie could only shrug and watch the four women as they reached the waterfront and began circling around the harbor. Emily in blue, Mom in a pretty sundress, and two women wrapped in the lightest shade of gold, lit by the morning sun until they shone.

Others in the crowd began noticing the approaching processional and quieted until the only sound was the bright ringing of the church bells. A narrow aisle was slowly forming through the heart of the crowd as people pressed aside.

"Archie, you're an idiot," Mark's whisper sounded fierce.

"Wouldn't surprise me," Archie kept watching Kee's approach and wondered how he should do it. Take her aside before the ceremony could start? And Dilya. How was he supposed to tell Dilya?

Mark snarled and grabbed his shoulder, forcing him to turn away. When he saw Mark's expression, Archie almost stepped backward off the breakwater and into the waves lapping directly below. Mark didn't look angry, he looked furious. His gray eyes had darkened until Archie wondered if he was about to be killed.

"Don't you *dare* do that to these women! That's a direct order, Captain Stevenson."

Archie kept his thoughts about civilian versus military spheres of control to himself.

"Shit!" Mark glanced up the breakwater where Kee and Dilya had disappeared into the back of the crowd.

Only the shining blonde of Emily's hair was high enough to show their progress through the gathered masses.

"I've got about thirty seconds, so just shut up and listen."

Archie shrugged his acquiescence. Nothing was going to change his mind, no matter how much it was hurting his heart. It was going to hurt Kee and Dilya, and it was going to kill him. But it was his job to protect them, even if it was from himself.

"I told you we've been feeling the pinch of not having you as the team's strategist."

"So?"

"Told you to shut up. I was going to tell you after your honeymoon. I structured the 5th Battalion D Company without an AMC. I didn't want some backfield, Air Mission Commander messing with my team—especially not some asshole who wasn't good enough to *fly* with my team. I built this company from the ground up and it only gets the best. That includes you, asshole. You're back in forward operations as fast as I can get you there. But you'll be flying in a command helo, well behind the line of fire, where you can direct the whole team."

Archie could only blink as his world shifted.

"You screw this up and Big John won't have a chance to pummel you because I'll beat the shit out of you myself. Do you understand me, soldier?"

Archie did. Not entirely, but enough that he managed a slow nod.

"You say one word other than 'I do' before this is over and I'll go from being your best man to your worst nightmare. You got that?"

"...I do," Archie managed.

Mark barked out a laugh, then slapped him hard on his bad shoulder.

Archie didn't flinch. It didn't hurt as much as he'd have expected.

He turned to face the approaching wedding party.

His mom and Emily led the way.

Dilya came next, in a modest dress, with leggings beneath and her favorite scarf covering her hair. There was the child of his heart. Someday he and Kee might have a child of their own, but it would be impossible to love it more than the war orphan that they'd be adopting as part of the wedding ceremony. The Chaplin had all of the official forms already prepared.

And then he saw Kee. Saw her and understood so much that hadn't been clear to him even moments ago.

She wore a dress of lightest gold that transformed her from the impossibly beautiful soldier to a glorious bride. It rode high up her neck, emphasizing the amazing line of her neck and strong shoulders. It hugged her generous curves proving that while she might be a warrior, she was also the embodiment of pure womanhood. A high slit in the long skirt revealed the occasional flash of her amazing legs, accenting Kee's inherent sexiness.

But there were two things that confirmed for him that he'd never have turned from her at this altar, even without Mark's surprising offer to rejoin the company.

Kee wore on her wrist the scarf that she and Dilya had purchased together. A connection so deep between the woman and girl. They were already family and it was breathtaking that they were letting him in.

The second was the color of the dress. It exactly matched the thin strip of Kee's dark hair that she always kept dyed bright blonde in memory of a friend who had been the one light in her ever-so-dark past. But now it was transformed. That tiny anomaly would now always represent her wedding dress and this day as well. It was absolutely transformative. How could he not love a woman who could pass through the trials she had and still let him all the way into her heart?

He broke Mark's mandate as she came to stand beside him before the Chaplin and whispered four words softly enough to be for her ears only.

"Night Stalkers Don't Quit."

She mouthed them back.

And looked at him with a third reason his next words would be "I do."

Just as on that first day, she looked at him with those beautiful dark eyes that showed all of her heart so clearly. That showed that she too would have sacrificed everything to protect their family.

Not because that was what a Night Stalker would do.

Because that is what a family did when the love was as true as theirs.

BONUS SCENE

This scene occurs during the story Kee's Wedding, but from Dilya's point of view.

Dilya knew something was wrong. The Kee never shouted, not even when she was very angry. Then her voice grew cold and dangerous as if she were made of ice. Dilya was always very careful to not anger The Kee. Dilya could tell when she was frustrated, but as she shared that feeling often herself, that didn't worry her.

Three and a half months ago, her parents had been killed and The Kee had climbed out of her helicopter to save Dilya when she had been starving to death in the cruel mountains called the Hindu Kush. In all the time since, The Kee had always watched over her—even held her close when the darkness had threatened to crush them both. And she had never shouted at Dilya.

But now The Kee stood in the hotel lobby and shouted so hard and fast that Dilya could not understand her.

Dilya and String Man—though it had been a long time since they'd played making string figures together—had come to Italy to become family with The Kee. Dilya was still struggling to understand why they had been apart. The String Man, who everyone else called Archie, had been shot and now had a new shoulder. Maybe that was why—The Kee had wanted to wait until he was repaired.

But that couldn't be right, because The Kee was always kinder than that. She wouldn't care that String Man was broken. She had said that she would become Mother and String Man would become Father when he was shot and The Kee's hands were still marked with his blood.

Dilya had understood so few words back then, but she would never forget those words. And she wouldn't ever forget the way The Kee had held her so hard it hurt, but Dilya hadn't cared because it felt so good too.

She had decided that The Kee had sent her to care for The String Man while he became better, so she'd done her best.

Dilya and String Man's mother, Calledbetty—who Dilya now understood was *called* Betty, but had insisted that Dilya not fix her name—had made sure he ate and did his exercises. Because his arm was in a sling, they couldn't play at string figures together, so she'd come up with other games that only needed three hands, not four. He had not smiled for a long time, but she had found ways around that too. Sometimes a pretty flower or leaf that she brought to him as if she didn't know what they were called. Other times she had him help her read *Winnie the Pooh,* though she could sound out most of the words and guess many of their meanings on her own now—even if the sounds were still wrong.

They still could understand so little of what the other said, though Dilya drove herself to learn English. It was so strange and foreign-sounding, like a Krait snake so tied in a knot that it didn't know it was biting itself until too late.

She did her best to memorize the sounds that The Kee was shouting so that she could think about them later.

"I was born on the streets. Mom took care of me when she wasn't too stoned to remember who I was. Marriage was something the judge did for people who somehow thought they'd last more than a year or two together. I sure never did. I can't be someone's wife. I *can't* be someone's mother."

But it was more than she could hold in her head and it slipped away even as she tried to memorize it.

Then it was all gone, except the last words.

Dilya could not swallow. Her throat hurt it was dry. She could not have heard those last words right. The English must be biting its own tail.

But The Kee's voice kept climbing louder and louder. Major Emily and Calledbetty tried to calm The Kee with words, but it didn't help. Though they spoke slower, Dilya couldn't concentrate enough to understand them.

They were all in their new dresses and all looked so pretty.

But pretty didn't seem to be enough for The Kee. Something more had upset her.

Dilya searched hard for the answer. Nothing must get in the way. She had to make sure that this time The Kee and The String Man became married peoples before one of them could go away again. Only then would she have a mother and father to replace her own. Hers had been shot so close by that she had worn their blood for many days until she found a freezing mountain stream to wash it away.

That must not happen ever again.

She thought back to yesterday in the dress shop.

The Kee had selected a dress for her wedding that was

so wrong. It was purest white and red. Everything about it was scary.

Dilya remembered the red cross on the white flag at the horrible refugee camp The Kee had taken her to. Dilya often wondered if The Kee had meant to leave her at that awful place where the stench of fear and despair had been so thick on the air it was impossible to breathe. But that was impossible—The Kee would never do such a thing. She had saved Dilya, protected her against so many things, she would never do that. But the horrid flag was burned into Dilya's memory.

And the dress' red trim had made The Kee look as if she was bleeding, sliced to pieces by a sword of justice, and not yet knowing that her body would fall apart in moments. The dress told so many wrong stories. It wasn't like Winnie the Pooh finding a honey jar...

That had given her an idea and she'd set off into the store to find the right dress. One that was Kee-sized and one like it that was Dilya-sized. She'd almost despaired, but finally had found them hidden behind by a dress of such bright orange that a person who wore it would look as if they were on fire.

But she *had* found them and The Kee now wore the perfect dress. It covered her so that Dilya could see she was so beautiful. The evil dress of white and red had made her hard to see, with all of her skin in the way. And the color was so perfect.

But still The Kee was unhappy.

Was it possible that she didn't understand?

The Kee held up Dilya's hand where it clasped The Kee's as if to prove something to Major Emily and Calledbetty. Dilya now knew the sound in The Kee's voice.

It was terror.

Dilya knew that sound too well, even if she didn't ever let it reach the outside.

She must try something.

Nothing must stop the making of her new family.

She tugged on The Kee's hand to make her kneel where Dilya could reach her hair.

"What?" The Kee's words were gentle and soft, as if all the fear was gone. But Dilya could see that it wasn't. The Kee's hard breathing still made her chest heave. Her eyes were dark and wide. Almost as if she wasn't home in them.

Dilya stroked her fingers down the golden stripe in The Kee's dark hair. Dilya knew that it held a special sadness. Dilya had thought about the special sadness she felt for her own mother. But their hair had been the same color, so she needed no other color to remember and be comforted.

A second time Dilya stroked the little bit of bright hair, and then the front of The Kee's dress. Dilya had found the dress that matched perfectly—honey-gold. It would give the stripe of special sadness a new meaning of special happiness.

But The Kee did not look down to see the color of her dress. Could not turn to see that it matched the stripe in her hair.

There was too much panic.

Already The Kee's attention was going away.

Not knowing what else to do, Dilya reached into her pockets. At first she didn't know what filled her pocket so much, and then she remembered.

She had woken this morning long before The Kee.

And there had been String Man, asleep on the couch. He looked so tired, but he was there. They were all together. It was so close now that she knew it must happen.

Yesterday had been so confusing. With String Man on

the beach. Then all together at the airplane and lunch, but then The Kee had sent String Man away.

But this morning, they were together again. That *must* mean something.

Dilya had put on her special dress and then dug around in her knapsack. She had pulled out her scarves. Dilya liked the way she felt like a flower whenever she wore them, but none of them were important enough for making a family.

She delved deeper and found the *rousari* headscarves that she and The Kee had gotten together in the Pakistani market.

The Kee wore hers so little, that Dilya decided that she had forgotten about it. But not Dilya. She had never owned anything so beautiful as their two scarves. So she had kept it until The Kee remembered.

It was one of her earliest memories. Not the buying with The Kee, but of her own mother. Before the wars and the hunger, she remembered sitting by her mother's loom as she wove them. She remembered her father taking them away and bringing back food—he must have been selling them. But most of all, she remembered her mother making them. Dilya had tried, but her hands were too small, too clumsy. And then the war had come and they had been chased away. The last thing Dilya had seen as her father carried her out of the house was her mother's loom. It was filled with the first part of a green and blue headscarf.

In the market with The Kee, she had seen these scarves that were so fine, it seemed as if only Mother could have made them.

This morning, she had buried her face in them as she'd sat in the corner of the bedroom, the only one awake. They didn't smell of her mother, they never had. But she could imagine her mother having made them so that she and her new mother would wear them one day.

She had folded them carefully and put them in her pocket so that her real mother would be there for the day she, String Man, and The Kee became a second family.

And now her hand closed about them and she pulled them forth.

The Kee's face softened the instant she saw them.

Dilya didn't dare look up as she carefully folded it into a narrow band. The Kee could not wear it to cover her hair or around her neck. No. It would break the story of the golden stripe of hair and the perfect honey-gold dress. But she could wear it on her wrist. Then Dilya could pretend that her real mother and her new one were somehow the same person.

Even if they were so different, they both loved Dilya. And she loved both of them, so it must be okay. She hoped so.

Kee took Dilya's scarf and tucked it over her hair. She didn't want her hair covered, she wanted to be like The Kee with all of her special sadness color showing as special happiness, but she let The Kee put it on her.

Then, as if she finally understood, The Kee brushed Dilya's hair clear of the scarf so that it flowed down over her back. She truly was Dilya's new mother.

She threw her arms around The Kee's neck and was held in turn as Calledbetty spoke something over them that sounded like a blessing, but Dilya didn't even try to understand the words as she held on.

Dilya would never forget her first mother, but she knew that she and The Kee were meant to be together forever.

Both in their special sadness and their special joy.

The Kee stood, calm now. Again holding Dilya's hand.

"Let's do this," The Kee told Major Emily and Calledbetty.

As they walked out the door, Dilya reached out with her other hand to brush her fingertips over the scarf on The Kee's wrist.

Yes. It was true, String Man, The Kee, and Dilya would never be apart again.

Even the church bell knew her joy and rang it out for all to hear.

CONNIE'S WEDDING

ABOUT THIS STORY

AFTER THE NIGHT STALKERS #3, WAIT UNTIL DAWN...

Night Stalker mechanic Connie Davis can fix anything—anything mechanical. On the brink of her wedding day, she wishes that family and relationships could work as logically as engines.

Big John Wallace knows family like he knows his heart—which totally belongs to Connie. So why is he the one scared spitless when facing the altar for Connie's Wedding.

INTRODUCTION

Connie's my sweetheart.

I don't know what else to say. She has both feet planted firmly on the ground, is utterly brilliant in her own odd way, and stronger than I could ever dream of being.

I've tried many different times to capture my wife in a character and Connie may be the closest I've come. My wife is no mechanic, her memory is not photographic, and they don't look much alike. But her core of inner strength and unquestioning support thrives in Connie.

1

"Who were you?"

"What are you talking about?"

Connie sat in the stopped car and waved helplessly out the windshield.

"Who was I?" Big John dominated the right seat of the rental car—he was broad-shouldered and tall enough to dominate any car, but this one was a squeeze. He squinted out the front windshield as if searching for a clue. Something Connie was lacking at the moment.

"No, I mean who was *I*?"

"Being even less clear than usual, Connie. And that's saying something, girl. You're Sergeant Connie Davis and I'm Sergeant John Wallace. We're getting married in two days. Pleased to meet you." He held out a hand as if to shake hers. Instead she grabbed onto it with both of hers and held on.

He was right, her thoughts were usually clarified and tested inside her head before she gave voice to them. Only around John did she ever let that barrier down. She'd try again.

"Six months ago, I was here at your farm for three days. It didn't look anything like this." The previously winter-barren Oklahoma fields now stretched out of view with wheat to the left and corn to the right. She'd never imagined that the four tall trees at the four corners of the cozy two-story farmhouse would be massively pink magnolias in mid-June. The wrap-around porch was embraced by roses in a thousand shades. "It all looks so...homey."

"It is home. That's why it looks that way. And we'd be there if you'd just drive that last couple hundred feet."

"But who was I then? I...ran away."

She'd left abruptly six months ago in the middle of a devastating loss for the family. Grandpa Wallace, Grumps, had died. And, not knowing what else to do, she had walked away.

No, she'd run.

Had she thought she was protecting the family by removing the obvious outsider? She certainly hadn't recognized that there was any more than sex between her and John. It wouldn't be until she was barfing out her guts from pure terror against the sides of the Stockholm Cathedral that she'd come to understand that.

Had she thought she was protecting her heart by running away? Instead, she'd run from the only man who recognized she had one. Another thing she hadn't understood at the time.

Instead she had wounded the man she'd been learning to love—the first ever in her life. Thankfully, John had forgiven her.

But would the rest of his family? Their texts said yes, but her heart—and nerves—were far less sure. They were now just a hundred feet down the gravel driveway and she didn't recognize it at all. The tall corn blocked her view of the barn where she'd rebuilt Grumps' tractor. The house and its massively blooming trees blocked the view of the orchard around back.

The only thing that made sense to her in the entire vista was John close beside her and looking worried.

She hadn't seen a single one of the family since that day she'd run, except for Big John of course. Their team had been deployed in Eastern Europe—on the types of missions that no one in Eastern Europe could ever know about. They had been working to delay the Russian expansion, but it was clear that they were gearing up to roll westward once more. It looked as if Ukraine and Syria were in their sights and there was only so much the Night Stalkers could do to slow them down—warning Ukraine of the dangers to their Crimea region was still proving pointless. Some missions had delivered pinpoint "insurgency" at critically tactical moments. Dozens of other raids had gathered intel that the Russians had fought to hide.

The drastic setbacks they'd delivered to the Russian Navy's plans to create a new fleet of aircraft carriers could also never be pinpointed to the Night Stalkers of the 160th SOAR.

Sergeant Connie Davis recognized herself as Connie the soldier. She was proud of the silent, fanatically driven, ace helicopter mechanic of the most successful company in the entire regiment. When Joint Special Operations Command, or occasionally even the President, needed to activate a company for a black ops mission, they tapped the 5th Battalion D Company.

"Too late to run," John murmured in her ear.

"No. It's not. We drove from Fort Campbell, Kentucky, we can drive back just as easily."

"I'd be a goddamn pretzel by then."

She considered her options. The driveway in mid-June was a tunnel of green that the setting sun was fast turning to gold. It was beautiful—and it was completely unnerving.

How could it be such a shocking contrast to the pure blue, winter sky she'd seen last December? She'd understood herself those three, cold winter days. Their bitter chill had fit her—an Army orphan. Those three days were the first she'd spent any time with a family since her slow-fading grandmother had died when Connie was sixteen. The first real family since her father had been shot down when Connie was twelve.

These lush fields and lovely farmhouse before her, so vibrant with life, were so foreign they could be alien. She didn't understand any of this at all.

A small figure in a bright sundress stepped out onto the porch. After shading her eyes, the figure waved.

"Now it's definitely too late," John teased her.

Connie had finally learned how to judge when he was teasing her with greater than ninety-four percent accuracy.

"Who's driving anyway?" She tried a riposte—which had less than a five percent success rate at stopping John, but she kept trying.

"Not you. We're just sitting our asses here. C'mon, honey. This boy wants to go home. That's Mama waiting."

"You're close enough to walk."

"Nope. Not giving you a chance to run."

"I won't." And she turned to look at him. How had she ever run from him the first time? He was such a good man and the way he looked at her, she could actually believe in herself. She had made the mistake of running away once— perhaps the greatest mistake in her life as it had almost lost her John. Never again.

"Maybe *I'll* be the one to get out and walk." And she'd

take the keys with her if it would leave him stuck so close to home but unable to get there.

"Too late for that, too."

"Why do say thaaa—" She finished the last on a startled cry as a truck horn blared out close behind her. Only her seatbelt kept her from banging her head on the ceiling.

John waved cheerily out the back window.

Connie checked the rear view just in time to see Paps climb down out of his big pickup. He strolled up to her window with the rolling gait of a big man—almost as big and powerful as John—before crouching down to face her. They might not be related by blood, but Big John certainly *looked* like Paps' son.

"Getting pretty close to the altar to be getting cold feet." Paps' grin was as infectious as his step-son's.

"It's impossible to have cold feet during an Oklahoma summer," she did her best to smile back.

"Summer?" He inspected the sky in surprise. "This ain't but June. Even so, June brides got no excuses for cold feet. Do they, John?"

"Not as far as I can see, Paps."

"I was worried about you being the one with cold feet." The voice, and a smack on the back of John's head, came in from the window on his side.

2

_____

JOHN LAUGHED AND SHOVED THE DOOR OPEN AS HARD AS HE could. It caught Tim Maloney in mid-crouch, knocking him head over heels into the corn.

"What are you doing here, loser?" John climbed out of the car.

They traded crushing hugs after Tim extracted himself from the stalks. "Figured you'd be the one likely to be getting cold feet. So, I flew in early to keep you in line. Paps picked me up. Tried to time it with your arrival. Good timing as always." He congratulated himself as usual. He and Tim had met in Basic Training and flown together for over a decade. He was the unofficial white-boy son in the Wallace household.

"Why in the world would I get cold feet?"

"Shit, bro, facing the big 'I Do,' especially with a hot chick like Connie? Figured you for a definite runner." Tim sent a wink to Connie where she was coming around the car.

She accepted Tim's hug, but John could see that she didn't quite know what to do with it. They were all Black

Hawk crew chiefs for the 5D. Connie had earned her place —no one doubted that, not even Tim since their first Ukraine mission. But she was still…Connie.

"Hot chick" was the wrong adjective. That's what he'd always gone for in the past. Hot women, tall, and partial to short dresses revealing legs that went on forever.

He looked at his fiancée.

Connie was the classic sitcom-girl-next-door: quiet, unexpectedly pretty with the softest light brown hair in the world, and gold-brown eyes so big that they seemed both innocent and filled with wonder all the time. He'd seen her in a blouse and skirt a grand total of once. She was a camo pants and t-shirt kind of gal who barely came up to his chin. She was also absolutely brilliant.

He'd been the Number One mechanic in all of SOAR until she came along and showed him how it was really done. Together, they kicked serious helo ass. Command had already started asking when they were going to leave the field and join the airframe development team. Not yet, but it *was* nice of them to ask.

"Man doesn't get this lucky twice in a lifetime, bro." Tim tried to trip him, but John had been watching for that. "You get that shit, right?"

"Don't I know it." John turned to Connie, because he still couldn't believe a man could get this lucky even once. Out of the corner of his eye, John saw Tim's attention drift for a second. He casually hooked a foot behind Tim's ankles and shoved him back into the corn.

"Now don't you two go wrecking our crops," Mama slapped a hand lightly against John's shoulder before she stepped into his arms.

All he could do was hold on.

This was what home felt like, exactly like this. She

smelled of the farm and his favorite peanut butter-chocolate chip cookies that she must have been baking pending his arrival. *She* was where he belonged.

Except that wasn't true anymore. He had two homes now.

And one stepped out of his arms to greet the other.

"Hello, Mrs. Wallace." Connie's shy setting was turned up full and he could see that her self-preservation blast shields were set for fast closure if needed.

"Oh, none of that now, Connie. Name's Bee and you know that right well."

"I do...Mrs. Wallace." Then Connie was actually the one to step forward into Mama's arms as Mama laughed.

John offered her an eye roll and Connie stuck her tongue out at him over Mama's shoulder. A very encouraging sign.

3

CONNIE DIDN'T UNDERSTAND. SHE HAD LEARNED TO ACCEPT that there were some things beyond her, but still it rankled that some portion of her was simply...missing, and she couldn't even see what it was.

She had hurt this family and herself in the process—though being a loner since Dad's death when she was twelve, that latter part didn't worry her. And yet John's family treated her as if the only curious thing she'd ever done was to get engaged to John. She was made welcome at the big kitchen table as if she'd sat there a hundred times, not three. Her offer to help with the dishes had been readily accepted as if she was family, not a guest.

It was incomprehensible.

As evening had turned into night, they'd all moved out onto the porch to sip beers and watch the lightning bugs dance over the back lawn. The talk wandered as lazily as the big fans which dissipated the heat and the mosquitos. It focused on the news of the farm, mostly what was being planted where and why. With Grumps gone, Paps had taken full possession of his role as farm manager and head of the family. The family discussed the changes he was bringing in. Nothing big, but there were some crops that had flourished in Grump's youth that were no longer as viable with the changes in seed stock, the weather, and the marketplace.

She had grown up on Army bases and lived and breathed helicopters. It was all a foreign language to her, though she could feel through the arm draped lightly about her shoulders John's nods of approval about the changes Paps had made. Tim and Larry were farther down the porch trading girl stories.

"Girls and cars. Same thing every time those two get together," John whispered to her.

"Do you miss it?"

His low chuckle said that she'd been right, that was his earlier place on the porch. He turned enough to kiss her on the temple.

"Got the best girl anywhere already. Don't see much point in revisiting any past that glows less than a lightning bug when you're shining brighter than a sun."

"Smooth talker."

"Must be how I won your heart." It was anything but that. Smooth talk was almost as mysterious to her as why alfalfa was preferable to corn in the southwest acreage.

Connie had never imagined herself living long enough to think about a man in more than the briefest of terms. And the few times she did, she'd imagined a quiet, studious engineer. Instead, Big John Wallace was at the center of every story and launched every laugh that echoed through their flight crew. He lived in a state of innate joy that poured forth in his booming voice and grandiose gestures. It had pushed her away; made it clear that she didn't belong anyplace near such gusto for life.

But he'd won her respect by being the finest mechanic she'd ever met. Eventually he'd won her love by...seeing her. By seeing her as she'd never seen herself; worthy of something more than fighting the good fight until some mission went horribly wrong and snuffed her out faster than one of the lightning bug blinks.

John, with a strong nudge from his sister, had given her a dream that lasted beyond the next mission. It was a gift she had never imagined.

He'd also given her a gift of family.

Yet another thing she still couldn't understand.

4

———

"HEY, KNOTHEAD."

John eased open one eye to see his sister glaring down at him.

"Hey yourself, Meddler. When did you get in?" Noreen was six-months into her Army training as a medic and it clearly agreed with her. She'd always been slender and the real beauty of the family, but now there was a shine to her that came from being Army fit and loving it.

"Just now. Where's Connie?"

"What?" He opened his other eye and looked at the pillow beside him. No Connie, though it still bore the impression of her head. Barely. It had been smoothed out. He remembered the awesome wedding reception morning wake-up sex, but had fallen back asleep afterward. She had—

Run again!

"Goddamn it! She said she wouldn't!"

He jolted out of bed.

Noreen covered her eyes. "Whoa! Too much information, big brother."

John flipped the sheet around his hips and struggled to reach his pants draped over the back of a chair while keeping himself covered, but it was tucked in too well on Connie's side. She'd, of course, made her half of the bed already—to full Army regulations—even with him in it.

"Ease the Code Red. Her gear is still here."

And then he spotted it. A small duffle bag, too small for any normal woman, but Connie wasn't normal. She was the queen of efficiency—even by Army standards. It still rested beside the dresser he'd meant to clear out for her last night, but forgot.

He sat back on the bed with a gasp of relief. Noreen had been almost as devastated as he was when Connie had left the farm so abruptly on Christmas Eve after Grumps died.

"I'm going to forego the hug until you get yourself dressed. Mama has breakfast waiting."

He sniffed the air. Eggs, bacon, and her own warmed sand-plum syrup which meant pancakes as well. Pure heaven.

"You ready for this, Slacker?" Noreen dropped down to sit on his clothes, knowing full well she was delaying his race to breakfast.

"Look, Trouble. I can't get dressed if you're sitting on my damn clothes."

She raised her butt enough to pull out one sock and tossed it to him before settling back down. "Better?"

"Way!" He pulled it on just to show her who was in charge.

"So answer the question."

"What question?" He knew damn well what question.

That earned him yesterday's underwear in his face. He slipped into them under the sheet.

"What makes you think I'm gonna screw this up? I love

her. I'm going to marry her tomorrow. Happily ever after will start immediately after the ceremony."

Noreen shrugged uncomfortably.

"What?"

"Don't know. Call it an itch."

"Shit. I'll track her down and ask."

Noreen scoffed at him just the way she used to when he'd bring a date home—one Noreen didn't approve of. It was her "You're so stupid" scoff. No way was he rising to the bait.

Or maybe he would. "What?"

"Don't you know anything about her? You hit her with a question like that and all you'll get is the blank mechanic look. You better let me deal with her if you want her to make it to the altar."

"You're saying you know more about my fiancée than I do?"

"Hello. *Woman* sitting here on your clothes. Can't help it. Besides, it's you. Larry's golden retriever knows more about women than you do."

"Can't you go bother Janice?"

"Oh, like I'm so close to her." Which was true. Of the four siblings, Janice and Noreen had never been close...at all. "But even she'd handle Connie better than you would."

"If I weren't still mostly naked, I'd whup your butt, Nori."

"I dare you to try. I double dare you."

John pushed off the bed to lunge at her, but she was too fast. Between one breath and the next she was gone out of the room.

When he turned to face the chair, he saw that his shirt and pants had gone with her. At least she'd left his other sock.

5

"HE'S GONNA KILL YOU." IF JOHN SAW CONNIE LEANING INTO the engine compartment of his pet GTO and tinkering, he just might. Even if they were engaged. He and Paps had kept it out in the barn and worked on it only when they were together. It had been one of their rituals since she was a little girl. It was never going to get done.

"Noreen!" Connie's look of delight was too big to fit on her face. And in the next instant, it disappeared back behind that ever-so-careful Connie wall.

"Hello! Happy to see you too."

"You really are?" Meek Connie asked carefully.

Noreen just laughed and hugged her. The fierceness of the return hug was shocking. It was very un-Connie-like. By the end of it, Noreen was discovering that she was feeling sniffly. Connie didn't hug her like her fiancée's sister; she hugged Noreen like they *were* sisters. Like twin sisters who had been apart for far too long, rather than two women most of a decade apart in age and who had met for three days. Three days that had ended in a funeral.

"I was so afraid that you'd be angry. I missed you so much," Connie mumbled.

"Me too." No matter how ridiculous, it was true.

Connie stepped back and leaned on John's precious car, shifting most of the way back into her usual self, though not all the way. No tears had run, but her eyes weren't any drier than Noreen's. There was a long silence as Connie gathered her thoughts, which Noreen had learned to wait through.

"And you've forgiven me for...you know?"

"Running out of here like a demon was chasing your ass?"

"Yes, that would be an accurate description. In several ways."

"Nothing to forgive. You're the one who finally convinced me I was doing something important and to hell with what anyone else thought." She tapped her collar where her lieutenant's bar would be if she was wearing her uniform. "I spend most of my days trying to figure out how to live up to *your* standard."

"My standard? I've spent the last six months trying to live up to yours."

Which set them both to laughing. Noreen knew so much about her, and also so little. It was awfully confusing. Which in Connie's neatly ordered world must be times a hundred.

So, Noreen sat down on an old milk crate in the corner.

"No! Don't!"

Noreen leapt to her feet and stared down at the crate to see if there was a giant milk snake or something.

"Sorry. I—" Connie studied the thin layer of straw on the barn floor.

"What?"

Connie just shook her head.

"Give, sis."

Connie eyed her carefully, "Promise you won't laugh."

Noreen crisscrossed her chest and held up a Girl Scout sign.

"When I rebuilt Grumps' tractor last Christmas, he would sit on that crate and watch me. I... It feels as if he's here with me if that crate is sitting there."

Noreen wasn't able to blink away the tears this time and soon they were both sniffling.

"He opened a hole in my world."

"Dying will do that. He loved you a lot, Connie. We all did. So fast."

"No, it wasn't his dying." Connie went over and straightened the crate so that it was angled just so.

Noreen could almost see him there—a big man that even age couldn't waste wholly away. His sparse tightly curled hair gone long past gray and into white. That easy smile that could welcome her home from a day at school as if she'd been away for a year or put her in her place with equal ease.

"It was his *living* that did it. He's the closest to family I've had since I was twelve."

"You're going to have a whole lot more tomorrow."

Connie offered a quirky smile, which was a new one on her.

"Maybe if I get this GTO running, I'll race out of here."

The car was in a kajillion pieces. The frame was there and most of the shiny black metal was back in place. And the engine was under the hood. But the hood was propped up against the barn wall and nothing was attached to the engine. Wires seemed to sprout everywhere. A stack of red leather interior panels were laid on a pair of sawhorses. The car itself was up on blocks with the tires sitting in the corner and no brakes or anything on the axles.

But if anyone could do it in the next twenty-four hours, it was her future sister-in-law.

"If you do decide to bolt, you've got to make me a promise."

"What?"

"Take me with you. Either that or I have to face a summer studying human anatomy."

"Deal!" They shook on it. "Can you give me a hand?"

And Noreen leaned in to work on the engine with the kind of sister she'd never had but always dreamed of. She didn't know a thing about engines, but she knew she was happier being close to Connie.

6

His plans to track down Connie—no matter what Noreen said—kept getting sidetracked.

Tim had been chowing down in the kitchen, which had turned into a long and friendly meal with Mama teasing them for being sleepyheads, the last awake. They'd all caught up with each other in ways they hadn't had time for last night.

As he finished washing the fry pan, Mama had given them a list for the grocery store, about a half million items long. So off to the local Homeland.

"It's weird buying groceries." John stared down the next aisle with some trepidation.

"How long since the last time you did this, man?" Tim asked as he stared wild-eyed at the cereal aisle. In an Army mess there were about five choices. At the normal forward operating base they were lucky to have a choice of one.

"A while," John glared at the list. Milk wasn't just milk, it was "two percent organic." Did that mean that only two percent of it was organic or... "Shit, man! It's been a long while."

"The Army provides."

It was strange. He hadn't had an apartment—ever. He'd gone from home to enlisted. Meals were dealt with. All kinds of civilian things were dealt with: no electric or water bills, no decisions about meals except whether to take the lasagna or the meat loaf. No question of even shopping at the PX for anything other than munchies, because no real point in keeping food around when you could be deployed on a moment's notice.

Connie had it even worse than he did, growing up as an Army brat. At least he could take care of this so that she didn't have to.

That didn't stop him from wishing she was the one stuck with this when they hit a produce aisle longer than the cargo bay of a C-17 Globemaster III jet transport.

"It's an issue, man," Tim agreed as they nosed their two carts into the vast array of greenery. "Feels like I'm doing an infiltration."

"It *is* an issue. How am I supposed to be the man of the family when I don't even know how to buy groceries?" Grumps had taken care of the farm into his eighties. Now Paps had taken up the reins and Larry would follow in his footsteps. Whereas he—

"Don't worry so much, bro. Connie is enough of a man for both of you."

He considered rearranging the lettuce display with Tim's head. She was certainly more woman than he knew how to deal with.

"At least she's not some weenie like you, Tim."

"Lame," Tim rated his comeback as they both stared at the carrots in dismay. The list said "carrots" but there was mini-peeled in a bag, full carrots in a bag, and a stack of loose ones two feet deep arranged in a neat stacked semi-circle with carrot butts facing them.

It *was* a lame response, but it was the best he had.

Tim pointed down the aisle to where there were more carrots still with their green tops and a sign above them that said organic. They finally took one of each kind of bag and a fistful each of the loose ones.

That's what they'd both always done: scooped up all kinds of willing ladies, had a great time, and let them go. Nobody pinned down Tim Maloney and Big John Wallace when they were in a target-rich environment.

"What the hell happened to me?" John stared at the eighty types of lettuce: head, bag, little plastic boxes marked spinach, or arugula. There were mixes, blends, hearts, and who knew what all. Even figuring out and eliminating the cabbages and cauliflowers (which took some doing) didn't narrow the target selection near enough.

"You stepped on the landmine of *luv.*" Tim drew out the last word like some British comedian.

He left the lettuce to Tim and moved down to potatoes. John had worked the farm as a kid, he understood potatoes. Russet, golden, red, mini, heritage...*Shit!*

The landmine of *luv* was about right. Every time he looked at Connie, it was impossible to look anywhere else. And when he touched her—

A hand rested on his arm. Long, fine fingers. He scanned up the tall, lean body into Jennifer's lovely face and even darker eyes.

"Johnnie," her soft voice evoking a thousand memories. They'd hooked up a number of times since their first real fling the night he'd quarterbacked the Muskogee High School Roughers to third in the state championship. If he was home on leave and she was between boyfriends, they'd heat up the dance floor at Clary's and then scorch the sheets.

"Hey, Jen."

"Didn't know you were back in town." Her hand still rested on his arm. He knew full well how crazy she could drive him with those lovely fingers.

"Just a couple days."

"You know my number."

He could only nod. The words just wouldn't come out.

She sashayed away, picked up an apple and bit down on it with her perfect white teeth that could nibble at him until he was sure he'd died and gone to heaven. Sex with Jen had always been amaz—

Tim slapped him hard on the back of the head.

"What?"

"You did *not* just look at that." Tim's eyes weren't following Jen's walk around the end of the aisle, instead he was glaring at John.

"Some history there, man. Good history."

Tim smacked him again, and this time he looked pissed. "What the hell is wrong with you, man? Do I even know you? Marrying Connie Davis tomorrow. Sound familiar?"

John covered his face, trying to scrub the image of Jen out of his mind. She'd been gunning for him on and off for over a decade. He'd been looking for something different— never once imagining it was a short, quiet, white chick like Connie.

"Why is she scaring the shit out of me?"

"Jen? 'Cause she's the finest land shark swimming." When Tim had visited, they'd often double-dated with one of Jen's nearly-as-sultry friends.

"No, Connie." Jen had always offered an easy laugh and

awesome sex. Connie had blown up his world and stolen his heart.

"Because you aren't stupid."

"You saying I'm stupid to marry Connie?" Normally those would be fighting words, but now he didn't even know.

"No, asshole. Smartest damn thing you ever did other than teaming up with me. I'm saying Connie is scary as hell. She looked at you with those big golden-browns and, *Bang!,* you were off the market. No woman should have that kind of power over a man."

But she did. She totally did.

"You're next, buddy," he thumped Tim on the shoulder.

"No way in hell is some dame gonna pin down this boy."

"Yeah?"

"No. Way."

"Got a fifty on that?"

"Done!" They shook on it. He should have made it a hundred. "Double if it's inside six months."

"Yes! Easy money."

Then they turned together to face the question of onions: sweet, white, yellow, red, shallot... *Shit!*

7

CONNIE HAD MOST OF THE GREASE CLEANED OFF IN THE shower. It would only take another couple hours to finish the GTO. She wanted to keep working on it, but Noreen had insisted that they had to stop.

"Reception dinner tonight."

"I don't have to go, do I?"

"It's for *your* wedding, sis-to-be." Noreen's smile had been merciless.

"But it *is* going to be small? Your mom promised."

"Small by Wallace standards. It's a farm wedding, been a long time since we had one of those, sis-to-be. Deal with it."

So, Connie scrubbed and worried. She wasn't good with people, but they seemed to like her anyway...eventually. And John loved her which was the only thing in her life that made sense. Why couldn't it be just her and John? They'd go back to his friend's steak house for dinner and make love in the USS *Batfish* submarine museum just as they had last winter. Then they'd—

"Now that's a sight I've been looking for all day." John swept open the plastic curtain around the tub.

He was so magnificent she couldn't speak. Stripped down, John was the most beautiful man she'd ever seen. Broad chest, powerful legs, and a smile that was all for her. She set aside the soap as he stepped in to join her. She wrapped herself around him as he closed the curtain and folded her against that lovely chest.

Here.

Here was where Connie the woman made sense—the only place. Her was where she came to life and the fears slipped away. She'd learned she could rely on that like her favorite 9 mm box-end wrench. John was her place of safety and security. A security she'd never known. Of all the people she knew, only John was even more reliable than a Black Hawk's T700 turbine, and even those needed care and maintenance.

Perhaps people were like that too. It was a reasonable hypothesis. She had spent much of the day with Noreen. Had she been teaching Noreen about electrical systems as they'd pulled new wiring through the GTO's frame together? Or had she been maintaining, even cementing their future sister-in-law relationship? Perhaps both?

She looked up to study John's face before she spoke.

"I love you, John." That she didn't say it often didn't make it any less true.

His smile bloomed as his eyes squeezed even more tightly shut. She now had a better understanding of his happy sigh that followed. She'd have to remember to say it more often.

She buried her face once more into his chest to reinforce her own happy sigh.

8

———————

Five a.m.

No one in their right mind got out of bed at five a.m. Actually, that was usually around the time that a Night Stalker *went* to bed.

The house was silent. John knew Paps and Larry would be waking up soon, but they were working a farm. Even on a wedding day, the farm didn't wholly rest. They only kept a few dozen head of cattle for milk and beef, so the chores wouldn't last long. He wondered if he should wake Connie. Last night something had shifted.

They'd made love—a happy ritual they both enjoyed. Huh! He hadn't even thought once about Jen since she'd swayed away. Just thinking about Connie erased any other woman from even consideration. Being in her presence made it hard to think of *anything* else—like how comfortable his old bed was and how nice going back to sleep sounded.

Wasn't that a surprise? That a quiet, self-possessed woman could do that to him. Be funny to watch Tim when that caught up with him. John made a mental note to not give him the least bit of a break when it happened—and to collect his hundred bucks when some woman took Tim down for the now-and-forever dance.

But what was it that had shifted with Connie last night?

The sex had always been amazing. The contrast of such a careful woman who was so uninhibited in his arms was a constant wonder and being in the family bathroom hadn't changed that at all. He wasn't even sure who had taken who. Connie didn't play power dynamics—no question who was in control when he'd been with Jen. Jen had always made him feel like a man. Instead, Connie made him feel like he belonged exactly where he was.

Last night, after the dinner so rich with family and laughter, she'd simply held him as they lay together. She'd held him so tightly that it was impossible to imagine her wanting to be anywhere else. They didn't make pre-wedding love, they'd simply held each other in perfect, silent contentment.

Any worries that she'd run away again were simply gone.

He twisted around to look at her in the first hint of predawn light that trickled around the curtains...except she wasn't there. Her pillow was smoothed and her side of the bed was tucked in.

He turned on a light and managed to blink through the glare enough to finally see that her gear bag was still in place beside the dresser. Then where the hell was she? She'd eluded him all yesterday—not that he'd ever really had a chance to go find her.

A low rumble kicked to life somewhere out in the night.

A rumble that he'd imagined any number of times, but hadn't heard in forever.

It was a triple-carbed Pontiac 389 V8.

It was *his* triple-carbed Pontiac 389 V8.

John scrambled out of bed. The woman was working on *his* GTO.

In moments he was dressed and standing at the open barn door. He'd arrived just steps behind Paps and could only stare aghast.

Connie and Noreen were sitting in the front buckets.

"Good morning. We were just headed out to the airport. Mark and Emily are coming in on an early flight." Connie dropped it into gear and rolled it out of the barn—the first time it had moved since he and Paps had pushed the aging rust bucket into the barn a decade ago. Now it was a black beast of a machine that shone with its perfection. He and Paps had hoped to finish it over the next couple times he had leave, but there hadn't been time to get near it this trip.

Connie and Noreen pulled on their mirrored shades against the sudden punch of the sun rising clear of the horizon.

Noreen waved happily as they pulled away.

"But—" he told the slight dust trail as the beautiful car and the two beautiful women spun away in a cloud of gravel and dirt.

Paps looked at him.

"I'm sorry, Paps. I told her last Christmas not to mess with it; that it was your and my project. She must have forgotten."

"Johnnie, you bring a mechanic into the family, you're going to have to live with the consequences. Besides, she asked yesterday if it was okay. Looked like she needed something to do. Just didn't think we were that close to done."

"We weren't. At least not for anyone less of a mechanic than Connie."

"Well, now that you're up, there's some milking and stall mucking to get done."

John's groan didn't save him. Begging off that it was his wedding day didn't seem likely to work any better. So, he followed Paps out to the cow barn and wondered at the miracle of a woman who had just driven away.

9

EMILY HELD OUT THE SUIT BAG AS SHE WALKED UP TO THE CAR.

"Thanks." Connie hadn't left it back at Fort Campbell intentionally. At least she didn't think so. Some part of her had been reluctant to think about the wedding? No. She'd been so worried about her lack of welcome at the farm that she'd forgotten about anything as trivial as the wedding and her dress uniform until she was halfway to Oklahoma. Simply a matter of memory stack overload.

Her commander had insisted it was no problem to pick it up when Connie had called. She still couldn't believe that Majors Emily Beale and Mark Henderson had come at all. She'd only given them an invitation because it seemed rude not to. They'd both responded yes immediately. Was it any wonder that the 5D was the best outfit she'd ever served with, having two such commanders.

"Your dress fits in there?" Noreen eyed the thin bag as Connie lay it flat in the GTO's massive trunk.

"My dress *uniform*. Easily."

"You're *not* getting married in your uniform."

Connie glanced over at Major Beale for support.

Emily shrugged, "I was married in a dress. So was Kee. But a uniform seems fine to me too. That's what I was going to wear before my mom brought a dress for me."

"So not!" Noreen looked furious.

"Well, I don't have a mom."

That chilled Noreen down several notches.

"All I have is my uniform." And it was enough for her. It always had been and it always would be.

"But the wedding is *all* about the dress."

"No, it's about marrying John."

"Aside from that," Noreen insisted. "It's *all* about the dress! My new sister is *not* going to marry my brother wearing a military uniform."

Connie thought they had come to a new understanding working on the car. And now Noreen was suddenly furious. What was wrong? Something spontaneous was going on that she didn't understand. Something bad was going to happen and she had no idea how to judge what it was.

Noreen yanked out her cell phone and dialed.

An airport patrolwoman came up and told her that they couldn't remain at the curb, this was a loading zone.

Emily and Mark settled in the back seat. Atypically, he was holding his peace and dutifully climbed in beside his wife. But nothing was going to move Noreen. She was as formidable as Major Beale in her own way.

Connie circled around the car, and pushed Noreen into the seat while she was waiting for someone to answer the phone. Connie circled back and offered an apology to the patrolwoman.

"She's right, you know. The dress...absolutely." Then the woman continued her patrol.

Connie slid in behind the wheel. She was just fine with

her uniform. It certainly defined who she was better than some dress anyway.

"Mama," Noreen yelled into the phone over the roar of a departing jet as Connie pulled them away from the curb and threaded back into the traffic. "Connie only brought her uniform. She doesn't have a dress."

...

"No, I don't think it's up to her. It's just not right. Where's a shop that we have a chance of finding something ready-made?"

...

"What do you mean 'just come home'? Didn't you hear what I was say—"

...

"Yes, Mama." Noreen snarled at her as she hung up the phone, "Just go home."

Between Noreen's mood and Connie's trouble speaking to Emily when there were other people around, the front seat was very quiet for the long drive back to the farm.

Once they were back at the farmhouse and introductions had been made, Bee Wallace shooed Mark away. "You'll find the boys and a cooler of cider and such around the back of the house. They're in the peach orchard."

Connie had fetched her uniform from the trunk and she stood on the ground between Emily and Noreen. Bee looked down at them from the top of the porch steps, fists on her hips.

"Well, miracle of miracles, my girl is right. You can't be getting married in a uniform. That's everyday wear, child."

"No, it isn't." Connie wore it for award ceremonies and not much else. She didn't get invited to weddings, was never anyone's date to a formal banquet. And it had no place in the field or hangar, which was where she was most comfortable.

"No matter. You just come inside and we'll get you fixed up."

Trapped, unsure of what else to do, she was herded inside between the women.

10

_____

"JOHN!"

"Hey Archie!" John greeted Archie as he came into the orchard.

"Expelled by the women?" Mark greeted their Air Mission Commander.

"No. I simply assessed that a male would be risking his life to so much as attempt entrance. Given an escape route, I deemed it the best angle of attack."

"To run away in full retreat!" Mark agreed heartily and handed him a cold beer.

"Damn straight."

Archie joined the circle.

Paps, Larry, and Tim were manning the grill—sipping beers and watching the charcoal slowly coming up to heat for lunchtime burgers because, well, someone had to. Mark and Archie dragged over a couple of the chairs from the pile they were supposedly busy setting up for the evening ceremony.

"How's he holding up?" Archie asked Mark.

"Shaking like a leaf if I judge properly."

"Am not." John's denial sounded unconvinced, even to his own ears. How could a man be nervous about marrying Connie? Just wasn't possible. No way. No how.

"Isn't easy, you know," Mark studied his beer. John noticed that though he been nursing it a long while, it was less than an inch down. God forbid Major Mark Henderson should ever lose the least bit of control.

"Nope," Archie agreed. His, at least, was a quarter down.

John set aside his empty quietly and didn't take another.

"We're all family men," Mark continued.

"Yeah, you're both married to amazing women." John couldn't argue that point. Emily and Kee? If he did argue, Mark and Archie wouldn't have to do a thing—either woman could execute him just fine on their own.

"You will be too, but that's not what I'm talking about. We all come from family. We know what it means. That's what makes it hard."

"Emily did too," John didn't know why he was arguing.

"Kee and Connie are both orphans."

"Couldn't find two more different women," John had a contrary streak going and decided to let it keep running. Archie's wife was a former street kid and a tough-as-hell outspoken sniper. But she had some kind of weird soft side around Archie and the Uzbekistani war orphan they'd adopted.

Unless...

"Did you two hitch up because of Dilya?"

Archie's look told him he was an idiot. No news there. His friend was sweet enough that he'd marry somebody if it meant protecting her. But that wasn't the point. There was no way to deny that Archie and Kee were electric together— like she was the explosive and he was the safety.

What did that make Connie and him?

Today, it made her the rational one and him the basket case.

"You're spooked because you get what family means," Mark concluded. "Connie doesn't."

11

————

"ARE YOU SURE?" CONNIE COULD ONLY LOOK AT HERSELF IN
the mirror in astonishment.

Mama Wallace—impossible to still think of her by
something as remote as her first name—had offered Connie
her own wedding dress.

"For my future daughter, absolutely. Was I ever so
slender and fine as you?"

John had showed her the photos. When she was
younger, she could have been Noreen's twin.

The dress was simple and elegant. A loose-pleated
sheath below the waist with an embroidered sleeveless top.
It was in the softest pink with an only slightly brighter pink
wide belt defining her waist.

"It's the dress I married John in, your John's father before
he was killed by that drunk driver. I was so in love. We had
less than a year together. I was too pregnant with John
Junior when I married Paps to wear more than a sundress—
which was okay, it took me time to learn to love him. But
this is the dress of a woman already in love. Are you in love
with my son?"

"Desperately." The spontaneous answer surprised her, but it didn't make it any less true.

"Then you are wearing the right dress."

Around her stood her new releations-to-be: Mama Wallace and Noreen. Also, the women of her team: Emily and Kee. Perhaps they were her old family? Had she already discovered family on a cold winter mission far behind Ukraine "friendly" lines, and somehow not realized it?

"Perhaps some day you'll lend it to your sister-in-law," Emily observed softly.

Connie looked at the shock on Noreen's face. Followed closely by the longing.

Connie reached out and took Noreen's hand. "A dress for Wallace women to get married in?"

Noreen could only nod. It was funny seeing Noreen unable to speak.

Looking back into the mirror, she knew it was right. She was about to become a "Wallace woman." Even though she'd decided to honor the memory of her father by keeping his last name, it wouldn't be the name of her children. They would all be members of the Wallace family. And if one was a girl, perhaps she too would wear this dress someday.

Dilya was there too. So ecstatic to be with "the women" that her limited English had mostly flown out the window. She made up for it by parceling out hugs at every chance. Spent for the moment, she leaned against Kee. Their looks came from completely different backgrounds: Uzbekistan and Kee's Latina-Asian mixture. But even the least glance couldn't hide that they were family.

Mama Wallace and Noreen, and soon Connie Davis. Two beautiful black women and a white chick. But she would be family.

Would her own children favor John's coloring or hers? It

wouldn't matter, but she was surprised that she felt an eagerness to know. They had agreed that children still lay out in the future, after their service with the Night Stalkers, but she could almost see that future family. And in the present?

"I have a family *now*."

"Aw, crap!" Kee and Noreen sniffled together. Mama Wallace hugged her from behind.

Major Emily Beale softened just enough to smile at Connie's reflection. "I was wondering when you would notice."

"It's a new concept."

"Family?"

"No, having one. I've wanted nothing more than family since I can ever remember. My dad did his best, but he was often deployed six months at a time. With no mother, it left me to dream of family. But for all my dreams, I never actually thought I'd be part of one."

"Wake up, Sergeant Davis. You're about to become even more a part of one. Any nerves?"

"No." And Connie's reflection agreed with her. There was nothing she'd ever wanted more in her life. "I simply never believed it could happen to someone like me. But it already has."

Emily actually hugged her lightly, careful not to wrinkle the lovely dress.

"You're only just starting. It gets even better from here."

12
———

JOHN STOOD BEFORE THE BOWER MADE OF TWO PEACH TREES whose boughs joined above them in a graceful arc. Mid-June, the fruit was already ripening. The Wallaces had come from far and wide for the wedding. There were forty or more relations here, not counting the children who ranged across all ages.

Connie had so few people here.

Tim was here for him—currently asking John where the hell the rings had gone. No chance John was falling for that gambit, especially since he could see the boxes bulging in Tim's suit coat pocket. And Mark would kill him if he actually screwed this up.

Two female Night Stalkers for Connie was all she had in the world—their severe commander and the lethal Kee. His heart ached for her.

There would be more for her. He'd make sure of it.

That was a promise that he'd make on this day of promises and vows. He didn't know how, but he'd help her find family until she was surrounded by them. Until she couldn't turn around without—

First came Kee. She was in her uniform of course, leading Dilya. Together they sprinkled rose petals over the grass path that led into the heart of the orchard. They must have devastated one whole side of the house to have so many—pinks, oranges, reds, and golds scattered across the green orchard aisle.

Next Mama came round the hedgerow of sand plums that bordered the orchard. She looked elegant in a simple lavender dress.

He tried not to let his attention drift from Mama's hug and kiss, but he couldn't help looking to see Connie.

But it was Noreen who came next. She was crying despite the huge smile on her face. Noreen always was a mush.

Emily followed her, looking resplendent in her uniform —wearing far more medals than should be possible for any one officer to be awarded. She didn't say a word as she moved to stand to the bride's side beside Noreen. She didn't need to speak, her stare told him exactly what would happen if he hurt one of her crew. The fact that he was also one of her crew was completely irrelevant. Connie had helped save Emily's life and paybacks would be hell if John didn't live up to the expected standards.

Then he saw Connie turn into the far end of the orchard. John barely saw Mark holding her arm as he walked her down the aisle.

Connie was radiant. Her hair had been left loose, with just a light band to make sure it stayed clear of her lovely eyes. The sleeveless dress showed both her power and her impossibly feminine beauty. It was...familiar.

It was... He glanced sideways at Mama.

Her infinitesimal nod confirmed his guess. He had seen it many times in one of his favorite photos—his parents, his blood parents' wedding photo. He looked to see Paps' reaction—for Mama and Paps were his real parents as assuredly as if he was Paps' son rather than his nephew. His response was to wrap his hands around his wife's waist from behind and kiss her hair as they both looked back up the aisle. Mama hadn't been able to afford a nice dress for the wedding, and always said it was proof of how much John Senior had loved her for buying her such a dress.

And now Connie was wearing it along with a radiant smile as she crossed to him.

Mark kissed Connie on the forehead, just like a father might. Then he shook John's hand and threatened him in a whispered tone, just like a father would. Of course Mark's words were trite compared to Emily's glare. And both were meaningless in comparison to Connie's straightforward look.

His new wife's trusting look.

John looked at Connie's smile and those lovely wide eyes.

Their commanders' threats, his mother's gift of the dress, Noreen helping Connie finish the GTO, even Tim's leaping to be Connie's champion in the produce aisle. She already had family in more ways than he'd ever understood. And she knew it.

As they turned together to face the family minister, he could see his own family in a new light. Perhaps for the first time he appreciated just how lucky he was.

Then he looked once more at Connie and he knew *exactly* how lucky he was going to be: for as long as they both shall live.

LAST WORDS

Lola LaRue's wedding to Tim is captured at the end of The Night Stalkers #4, *Take Over at Midnight*.

That seemed a fitting closure to the four-wedding arc.

Except for one small detail. Emily, Kee and Dilya, and Connie each managed to show off their dresses on their story covers. Lola never had the chance. Well, Lola's dress, a flowing fantasy of brilliant lavender is on the cover of this collection.

DON'T MISS THESE GREAT COLLECTIONS

IF YOU ENJOYED THAT, DIVE INTO…

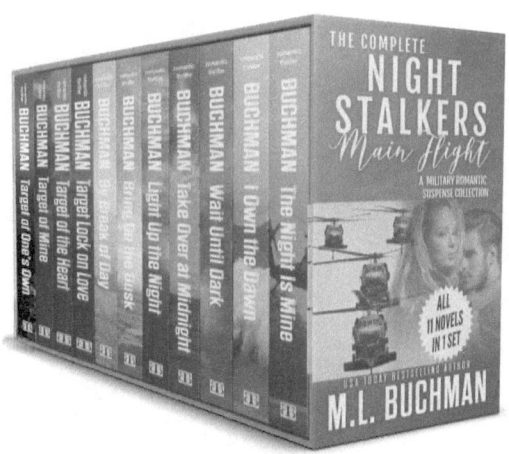

...and more at mlbuchman.com

ABOUT THE AUTHOR

USA Today and Amazon #1 Bestseller M. L. "Matt" Buchman began writing on a flight from Japan to ride his bicycle across the Australian Outback. Just part of a solo around-the-world trip that ultimately launched his writing career.

From the very beginning, his powerful female heroines insisted on putting character first, *then* a great adventure. He's since written over 70 action-adventure thrillers and military romantic suspense novels. And just for the fun of it: 100 short stories, and a fast-growing pile of read-by-author audiobooks.

Booklist says: "3X Top 10 of the Year." PW says: "Tom Clancy fans open to a strong female lead will clamor for more." His fans say: "I want more now...of everything." That his characters are even more insistent than his fans is a hoot.

As a 30-year project manager with a geophysics degree who has designed and built houses, flown and jumped out of planes, and solo-sailed a 50' ketch, he is awed by what is possible. More at: www.mlbuchman.com.

Other works by M. L. Buchman: *(* - also in audio)*

Action-Adventure Thrillers

Dead Chef
One Chef!
Two Chef!

Miranda Chase
Drone*
Thunderbolt*
Condor*
Ghostrider*
Raider*
Chinook*
Havoc*
White Top*
Start the Chase*

Science Fiction / Fantasy

Deities Anonymous
Cookbook from Hell: Reheated
Saviors 101

Single Titles
Monk's Maze
the Me and Elsie Chronicles

Contemporary Romance

Eagle Cove
Return to Eagle Cove
Recipe for Eagle Cove
Longing for Eagle Cove
Keepsake for Eagle Cove

Love Abroad
Heart of the Cotswolds: England
Path of Love: Cinque Terre, Italy

Where Dreams
Where Dreams are Born
Where Dreams Reside
Where Dreams Are of Christmas*
Where Dreams Unfold
Where Dreams Are Written
Where Dreams Continue

Non-Fiction

Strategies for Success
Managing Your Inner Artist/Writer
Estate Planning for Authors*
Character Voice
Narrate and Record Your Own
Audiobook*

Short Story Series by M. L. Buchman:

Action-Adventure Thrillers

Dead Chef
Miranda Chase Origin Stories

Romantic Suspense

Antarctic Ice Fliers
US Coast Guard

Contemporary Romance

Eagle Cove

Other

Deities Anonymous (fantasy)
Single Titles

The Emily Beale Universe
(military romantic suspense)

The Night Stalkers
MAIN FLIGHT
The Night Is Mine
I Own the Dawn
Wait Until Dark
Take Over at Midnight
Light Up the Night
Bring On the Dusk
By Break of Day
Target of the Heart
Target Lock on Love
Target of Mine
Target of One's Own
NIGHT STALKERS HOLIDAYS
Daniel's Christmas*
Frank's Independence Day*
Peter's Christmas*
Christmas at Steel Beach
Zachary's Christmas*
Roy's Independence Day*
Damien's Christmas*
Christmas at Peleliu Cove

Henderson's Ranch
Nathan's Big Sky*
Big Sky, Loyal Heart*
Big Sky Dog Whisperer*
Tales of Henderson's Ranch*

Shadow Force: Psi
At the Slightest Sound*
At the Quietest Word*
At the Merest Glance*
At the Clearest Sensation*

White House Protection Force
Off the Leash*
On Your Mark*
In the Weeds*

Firehawks
Pure Heat
Full Blaze
Hot Point*
Flash of Fire*
Wild Fire
SMOKEJUMPERS
Wildfire at Dawn*
Wildfire at Larch Creek*
Wildfire on the Skagit*

Delta Force
Target Engaged*
Heart Strike*
Wild Justice*
Midnight Trust*

Emily Beale Universe Short Story Series
The Night Stalkers
The Night Stalkers Stories
The Night Stalkers CSAR
The Night Stalkers Wedding Stories
The Future Night Stalkers

Delta Force
Th Delta Force Shooters
The Delta Force Warriors

Firehawks
The Firehawks Lookouts
The Firehawks Hotshots
The Firebirds

White House Protection Force
Stories

Future Night Stalkers
Stories (Science Fiction)

The Emily Beale Universe
Reading Order Road Map

any series and any novel may be read stand-alone
(all have a complete heartwarming Happy Ever After)

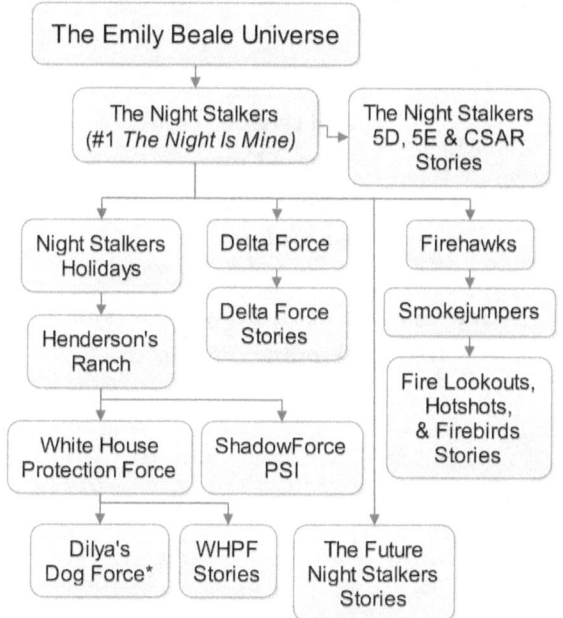

The Emily Beale Universe

The Night Stalkers
(#1 *The Night Is Mine*)

The Night Stalkers
5D, 5E & CSAR
Stories

Night Stalkers
Holidays

Delta Force

Firehawks

Delta Force
Stories

Smokejumpers

Henderson's
Ranch

Fire Lookouts,
Hotshots,
& Firebirds
Stories

White House
Protection Force

ShadowForce
PSI

Dilya's
Dog Force*

WHPF
Stories

The Future
Night Stalkers
Stories

* Coming soon

For more information and alternate reading orders, please
visit: www.mlbuchman.com/reading-order